my brother's hero

my brother's hero

ADRIAN FOGELIN

PEACHTREE
ATLANTA

A Peachtree Junior Publication

Published by
PEACHTREE PUBLISHERS
1700 Chattahoochee Avenue
Atlanta, Georgia 30318-2112

www.peachtree-online.com

Text © 2002 by Adrian Fogelin

First trade paperback edition published July 2005

Book and cover design by Loraine M. Joyner
Book composition by Melanie M. McMahon

Manufactured in the United States of America
10 9 8 7 6 5 4 3 2 (hardcover)
10 9 8 7 6 5 4 3 2 1 (trade paperback)

Library of Congress Cataloging-in-Publication Data

Fogelin, Adrian.
My brother's hero / Adrian Fogelin.
        p. cm.
Summary: Thirteen-year-old Ben is annoyed by an eleven-year-old, know-it-all girl who threatens the fun of his family's vacation in the Florida Keys, but he has other worries, especially anxiety about his friend's reaction when she opens the gift he gave her for Christmas.
        ISBN 1-56145-274-2 (hardcover)
        ISBN 1-56145-352-8 (trade paperback)
        [1. Interpersonal relations--Fiction. 2. Family life--Florida--Fiction. 3. Vacations--Fiction. 4. Christmas--Fiction. 5. Florida Keys (Fla.)--Fiction.] I. Title.
PZ7.F72635 My 2002
[Fic]--dc21

                                                    2002004833

Visit the author's website at
www.adrianfogelin.com

*For my husband, Ray Faass, best friend, sweetheart,
and occasional catcher of tarpon using odd lures.*

*To my agent Jack Ryan, publisher Margaret Quinlin,
editor Vicky Holifield, and the whole Peachtree family, thanks for helping
my stories grow up to be books.*

*Thanks, as always, to my friends and critics,
the Wednesday Night Writers.
You guys don't let me get away with anything!*

contents

PECANS FOR CASH

ow listen up. I found us a few new places." Nana Grace flat-tened the little map she'd torn out of the phone book against the hood of the truck. "There's a mess of pecan trees on St. Augustine." She gripped the pencil and drew an X. "That's where we'll start. Okay, Ben?"

I stifled a yawn. "Sounds good," I said. I had done my job by get-ting out of bed at six-thirty on a Saturday morning. Like all the kids standing around the truck, I was just waiting.

Leroy slow-bounced a basketball.

My little brother Cody stood on one foot, trying to set a new world's record. "How long was that, Ben?" he asked when he put his foot down.

"Oh, 'bout twenty-two seconds," I told him.

Cass was hugging herself, trying to stay warm inside her thin windbreaker.

Jemmie leaned over to scratch an ankle. Of the eight kids waiting to pile into the truck, Jemmie Lewis was Nana Grace's only real grandkid. The rest of us were honorary.

"My, my," Nana Grace likes to say when we're all hanging out on her big front porch, "don't I have me a *fine* lookin' mess of grand-babies?"

We're a mess all right. Black, white, short, tall, fat, thin, different ages. We all have real grandmothers we see on holidays. Nana Grace is for the rest of the time. Until a cop makes her turn in her license for driving bad or for being too short to see over the wheel—or until one of us gets wheels of our own—we'll ride around in the back of her pickup.

"An' then we'll swing by those big old trees near Railroad Square." Nana gouged another X into the paper. "All that'll take about an hour."

Justin groaned.

Nana Grace looked at him sharp. Slumped against the truck, his shirt hung out. He was staring at his untied sneakers. "You got a problem, Justin?"

"He stayed up 'til three playing video games," Clay reported.

"Three-thirty," Justin croaked. "Go easy on me."

"Easy my foot. We got pecans to get." Nana Grace liked us—but she didn't treat us soft. She drew another X. "After that, we'll check out Meyer's Park." She looked up and caught me in the middle of a really big yawn. "How 'bout you, Ben? You get your beauty rest last night?"

"Yes, ma'am. But what would it hurt to start a little later?"

"Wouldn't be a nut left on the ground if we slept in. Those old men with paper sacks'd pick up every last one. No, Ben. You gotta be the early bird." She dropped the pencil in a sagging sweater pocket and snatched the straw hat off the top of the cab. "Everybody in back. Hustle, now!" And she jammed the hat down to her eyebrows.

Cass and Jemmie stepped onto the tailgate and Clay scrambled up behind them. He turned to Justin, who was puffing, one knee on the gate. "Hey, lard-butt, need a hand?"

I climbed up, then grabbed my brother by the seat of the pants and lifted. Last year Cody was too little to go after pecans. He was still too little to be any real help, but he begged. Dad made me promise to keep an eye on him. "You sit over here," I said, putting him on the girls' side with Cass and Jemmie.

"You two waiting for a personal invitation?" Jemmie called to Leroy and Jahmal. The brothers stood in the driveway, bounce-passing the ball. Leroy was the holdout. Jahmal was only following the lead of his big bad brother.

Leroy spun the ball on one finger. "Mr. Cool?" Nana barked from the driver's seat. "'Less you wanna get left behind, you'd best move your feet." With a belch of smoke we began to roll.

The ball sailed into the truck, followed by the brothers. I jerked the tailgate up. Leroy plopped down next to Jemmie and slid his foot over until his sneaker touched hers.

She glared and pulled her foot away, then whispered something in Cass's ear. The girls giggled.

"Hey!" Leroy held up his hands. "It was an accident, okay?"

Cass whispered something to Jemmie. They giggled again. The two girls were like yin and yang. Cass was white, Jemmie black. Cass quiet, Jemmie in-your-face. But together they made some kind of weird whole.

"Bet you're talking about us," Clay called over to them.

Jemmie rolled her eyes. "In your dreams."

All the guys were dying to know what those two whispered about us—and scared they didn't talk about us at all.

Nana Grace popped a wheelie turning onto Roberts Avenue. We all slid. Just as quick, she whipped the wheel the other way and stomped the gas.

"I steered better'n that when I was ten," I shouted in Clay's ear.

"Ten?" As the wind picked up, Clay's red hair began to whip around like his brain was on fire. "Come on. You're lyin'."

"I swear. Dad took me parking-lot driving on my tenth birthday."

In just eighteen months I'd have my learner's permit. Then maybe Nana Grace would slide over and let me take the wheel. I was tired of being a rider.

I hung my elbows over the side of the truck. In a second, Clay slid closer to me and did the same. "Hey," I shouted. "You mind getting out of my lap?" And he backed off a little.

Justin sat off by himself, facing the tailgate. Lately, he'd been saying things like, "Ben, did you ever wonder what it's like to be dead?" Sometimes he scared me.

"You're just gettin' your weight first an' your height second," Nana Grace had told him. But that didn't help when short, fat, and zitty was what he was right now.

Leroy stretched his long legs out, then glanced over to see if Jemmie was impressed. I kept my own legs bent. Until last summer I was the tallest guy in the neighborhood. But these days, when it came to tall, Leroy was the man. "Three and a half inches since summer," he brags to anyone who'll listen.

Seeing him over there relaxing, eyes half-closed like a lizard, it was easy to tell he felt good about himself—good enough to deny Jemmie Lewis's existence.

I checked Jemmie to see if he was getting to her but ended up looking at Cass. Her short, brown ponytail was blowing to one side. Her freckles looked like somebody'd spilled cinnamon all over her. I wondered if they went up under her hair, the way some dogs' skin is spotted under the fur.

She and Jemmie hugged their knees to stay warm. I bet Leroy was thinking about putting his arm around Jemmie. Thinking, not doing. I looked over at Cass, but we weren't like that. We were buddies. In fact, if you asked me who my friends were, I would've named the guys in the truck: Justin, Clay, and Leroy. We hung out together, we messed around, we killed time. But my real best friend out of every one in the truck was Cass—even though you would've had to cut my tongue out before I'd say it.

Me and Cass have known each other since we were both babies. Her mother has pictures of us taking naps in the same playpen— another thing I'd never talk about.

Cass wiggled the fingers of one hand, sending me a secret wave. She smiled and the corners of her eyes crinkled up. I smiled back. Then we both looked away. Too bad Cass is a girl. People get the wrong idea.

When I glanced at Cass again, Jemmie caught me looking. She scooted closer to Cass, squeezing out the last air molecule between them. After that, I did the lizard thing with my eyelids. When did everything get all boy-girl weird?

I felt tired, and it wasn't just getting up early. I was tired of doing the same old things. Like the pecans. We went after pecans every year. If Cody hadn't threatened to stink me out with a giant fart, I would've stayed in bed this time.

I wanted to *do* something. But being thirteen and a half isn't about doing, it's about waiting. Waiting to get a license. Waiting to get a car. Waiting around.

I looked at Cass between half-closed lids. When I finally got that license and car, when I finally went someplace, maybe she could ride along.

Thwomp. Nana Grace rolled two tires up on the curb and set the hand brake. "I know what you're gonna say, Ben," she yelled back at me. "But I don't trust the crazy drivers in this town."

"Nobody's up but us, Nana Grace," I shouted back. "No one in the whole city of Tallahassee. We beat the old guys by hours."

Her door opened with a loud creak. "It don't pay to waste daylight." She climbed out and stood in the street. Her stockings were rolled down below her knees, her hat crooked. "Let's move, folks!" And we all bailed out of the truck.

She passed out paper bags. We carried them up and down the street, collecting pecans from the sidewalks and gutters and the edges of lawns. Just last year this had seemed like fun. Now I kept wondering about the people inside the houses. What did they think about having a swarm of kids running around snatching nuts off their driveways?

Nana Grace walked like she had screws in her knees, cranked half a turn too tight. Cody nearly bumped into her as he hopped by on one foot. "Whatever are you doing, child?" she asked, dropping the pecan she had just picked up.

"Not stepping on cracks!"

"Not pickin' up nuts either." But I noticed she was smiling. "People," she called to the rest of us. "Y'all go for the big ones this time. Ashmore's don't hardly pay squat for the little ones."

I looked up into the trees. The last rain had brought most of the pecans down. We were about out of Saturdays to gather pecans for cash. Just five more school days, and we'd be on Christmas break. Not that it would be much—two weeks of pick-up basketball on the middle school playground. The hoops there were so low I could slam-dunk without even jumping. We'd ride bikes, hang out, try to talk some adult into driving us to the dollar movies or the mall.

Christmas morning, everyone would show off their loot—everything but the socks and underwear. Then we'd go back to shooting hoops or riding bikes—the same old stuff.

I was picking up a little pile of nuts that had washed together by the curb when Nana Grace swung her stick over her head. "Back in the truck, people! We've about picked this place clean." Everyone scrambled. And we headed for the next X on the map.

The old men showed up around ten. Old women too, plus a few kids, everyone gathering pecans. Nana gave me a look. "See what I'm talkin' about, Ben? You got to be the early bird if you're pickin' up pecans for cash."

It was almost noon when Nana Grace yelled, "Payday!" The old pickup's tires squealed against the curb in front of Ashmore's.

She kept one bag of nuts for pies. "My share of the haul," she said. She had Mr. Ashmore put them through the machine. While the machine ka-chunked, the kids fanned out, poking through piles of junk and antiques. Ashmore's has been in the same spot fifty-three years. Some of the stuff looks like it has too.

Nana Grace held a flowered teacup in one hand, an old postcard in the other. "Got a little bit of everything here, don't ya?" she yelled as the pecans rattled down the chute.

"Yup," Mr. Ashmore shouted back. "Better'n any ol' WalMart."

Clay carried the sack of cracked pecans to the truck. The machine didn't take the shells off, just cracked them. We'd be up on the Lewis's porch all afternoon picking shells.

We sold the rest of the nuts. The shrimps we should've left on the ground in the first place went for twenty-five cents a pound. "For that kinda money it ain't hardly worth bendin' over to pick 'em up," Nana Grace mumbled. Jumbos sold for seventy-five.

While Nana Grace divvied the money up on the truck hood, a couple of old men shuffled past, hugging sacks of pecans. Mr. Ashmore held the door. "Gentlemen," he said.

Nana Grace slid two dollars and seventy-two cents at each of us. "Y'all done good," she said.

Justin stared. "I fell out of bed for *this?*"

"You got a pecan pie coming too, if you bring yourself back by the house after lunch and help pick the shells off." When he still didn't take the money she said, "More for the rest of us," and reached for his share.

Justin scooped it up and stuffed it in his pocket. "But don't count on me for after lunch," he said.

"Suit yourself," Nana Grace told him.

But he'd be there. We'd all be there. It wasn't like we had anything better to do.

chapter two

ASTEROIDS AND ALIENS

Cody jangled the money in his pocket as we walked toward home. "Hey, Ben, I got an idea. Let's eat quick, then go to Mr. G's. Bet I have enough for a jumbo bag of chips."

I scruffed his short hair. "You know chips aren't on the Mom-approved list."

He skipped ahead of me, backwards. "But I earned the money myself."

"You got your Christmas shopping done?"

"Well, no." He kicked a ball lying in our front yard, sending it rolling toward me across the grass. "Whaddya think we'll have for lunch?"

"Peanut butter sandwiches with sprouts, same as always." I stopped the ball with the side of my foot and soccer-kicked it back to him. I wished an asteroid would drop out of the sky. I wished we'd be abducted by aliens—anything for a change.

"You forgot carrot juice." He chased the ball. "We always have carrot juice." He took a wild kick. The ball bounced off the storm door, making the glass shiver. "Oops."

"Man, you are so lucky you didn't bust it!" I jumped up and slapped the edge of the roof.

Cody raised an arm. He was too short to slap the roof by himself. "Lift me up, Ben!" I squeezed the back of his neck and shoved him through the door.

I slammed right into him when he stopped in his tracks just inside the door.

"What's going on?" he whispered. Dad, who is kind of chunky and no great dancer, was waltzing Mom around the living room, bumping into furniture.

"I guess they finally lost it," I whispered back.

Mom held her long skirt up with one hand. "We're going," she called as they whirled into the kitchen.

"It looks like you two are already gone," I called back.

"Was that sarcasm?" Dad asked as they reappeared in the kitchen door.

"It was," said Mom. "Let's leave him home." They spun into the living room, Dad's ponytail flying—and ran right into the couch.

"Hey, time out," I said, making a T with my hands. "Is this for real? Are we *really* going somewhere?" She smiled and nodded, but didn't say a thing. "C'mon, Mom. Dad, where are we going?"

"I need a drum roll!" Dad said, dipping Mom so low her long hair brushed the floor. Cody drummed his hands on the coffee table. "We're going to Bert's Marina!" Dad pulled Mom back up and put his cheek against hers. "Your aunt and uncle won a cruise! We're going to watch the marina for them."

"Christmas in the Keys!" Mom added. "What do you boys think about that?"

"You mean it?" I asked. "Christmas in the Keys?" I pumped a fist. *"All right!"* This was unprecedented! Colossal! Me and my brother wouldn't be hanging out on Magnolia Way this Christmas. We'd be at the other end of the state on an island that dangled off the tip of Florida like a lure on a fishing line.

Cody tugged my arm. "What's it like there, Ben?"

"Well, it's real bright." I tried to remember more. "And there's a lot of water."

He hung on my arm. "And what else?"

"Give me a break. I was only four when I went. There were kids all over the place. Everybody lived on boats." The other thing I remembered was looking up at Uncle Bert's big belly. That was basically it—sun, water, kids, and Uncle Bert's belly.

"Ben!" Cody squeezed my arm hard. His blue eyes bugged out. "Does Santa know about the Keys?"

"Sure, bro. He comes in on water skis."

"But…but…don't the presents get wet?"

All the kids from the pecan run were on the Lewis's front porch—plus Anna. Anna is like a distant moon that sometimes circles the planet Cass/Jemmie. Today her arm was around the neck of a dog that looked like it had been blown apart and put back together again—only missing a couple of parts. "You don't understand," she was telling Clay when me and Cody walked up. "They were going to put her to sleep. We *had* to adopt her."

"Couldn't you at least find a dog with two whole ears?" Clay asked.

The arm around the one-eared dog tightened. "No!" Anna had had a hard time finding a home herself. She was about to lose her foster home placement when Miss Johnette came to the rescue. Miss J is a biology teacher who lives in the neighborhood. They make a great pair. From bugs to ugly dogs, they both love nature.

"Hey there, girl." I said to the dog as I scratched her neck. "You got a name yet?"

"Her name is Beauty!" Anna nuzzled the patch of white on the dog's neck, then looked up and smiled. "Want to smell her? She smells really good." Cody took a whiff. "Just think," Anna crooned, hanging on her new pet, "when I woke up this morning I didn't have a dog and now I do! You never know when something good'll sneak up on you."

"Yeah!" Cody blurted out. "This morning I wasn't going on a trip, but now I am!" Everyone stopped picking pecan shells. "Christmas in the Keys!" For a minute they all sat, opening and closing their mouths like Justin's pet goldfish, Xena.

Things got so quiet, I heard a *ping* when Nana Grace dropped a shelled pecan into the metal bowl between her knees. "Well, now," she said. "Isn't that nice."

"You're leaving?" Cass asked in a small voice, her eyes on me.

"Yeah." I took a kick at the bottom step. "We have to help my aunt and uncle." Suddenly I didn't feel as good about going. Except for the one week a year her family visited her mom's folks in Georgia, Cass never went anywhere.

Maybe I could invite her along. My parents think the world of Cass. But I knew it wasn't going to happen. On the other side of the fence that divides the Bodine's yard from the Lewis's, her dad was on the roof, propping up reindeer. Christmas is a big deal at her house— the only big deal of the year. Besides, invite a girl on a trip? The guys would never let me live it down.

Cass was still looking at me. "Will you be gone the *whole* two weeks?" she asked.

"Yeah, pretty much."

"And guess what?" Cody whooped. "Santa's gonna come in on water skis!"

"Will you stay in Key West?" Anna asked.

"No." I scratched Beauty's neck, working my fingers down into the fur. "My uncle built his marina close to the mainland so they could get off fast if there was a hurricane."

"Key Largo?" Anna guessed. "Islamorada?" Anna's other hobby is maps.

"That's right, Islamorada." I liked saying it. Islamorada. Isla, like island. Morada, like...well, like something mysterious.

"Islamorada," Cass echoed. "It sounds so far away."

"It's still in Florida," I told her. But it was a whole different Florida. It was the Florida of hurricanes and pirates, of shipwrecks and sharks. The Florida where things happen.

"Well, 'til you get there, you mind doin' these, hammer-man?" Nana Grace pushed a bowl of pecans my way with the toe of her sneaker. Sometimes the cracker doesn't crack a nut enough. When that happens, I whomp it—Nana Grace gives me any job that calls for a tool. "Hammer's up on the windowsill," she said.

"Yeah, I know." I'd put it there myself the week before.

I hammered nuts on the top step and daydreamed about the trip. Every now and then Beauty would lick my neck with her pink-and-black tongue and bring me back to earth. Then I'd look at Cass. Seeing her picking bits of shell off nuts, I felt lousy for being so happy.

But it wasn't my fault. Like Anna said: sometimes good things sneak up on you.

"I'm going to New Leaf." Mom had the car keys in her hand. "Do either of you boys want to come?"

"Sure," I said. "I'll go." New Leaf is the natural food store where Mom buys tofu and mung beans and soy burger mix—things that would disgust the average kid who hadn't been raised on them. But I wasn't riding along to scoop things out of bins.

"I'm going to Crystal Connection," I said as Mom parked. "Christmas mission."

Her eyes sparkled. "Something for a girl?"

I handed her the canvas shopping sack she uses to save trees. "Yeah, Mom. You."

I pushed the shop door open. Chimes rang. I plinked my finger against one of the hanging prisms in the front window. The rainbows that dotted the walls went flying. "Can I help you?" asked a girl with eyebrow rings and a patch of purple in her hair.

"Just looking." I shoved my hands in my pockets and peered into a jewelry case. I don't normally look in jewelry cases. If something's in a case, I can't afford it. But it was Christmas, and I wanted something good for Mom.

Dragons, wizard rings, and crystals of power were arranged in rows. Most of the tags were flipped over. I squatted and tried to read them through the underside of the glass shelf, but it was hard. The ones I could read were pretty steep. I was about to check out incense burners when something at the very back of the case caught my eye.

Hanging between wizard and angel pendants was a fairy with dragonfly wings. In her hands she held a pearl, hopefully fake, if she was going to be anywhere near my price range. For some reason she reminded me of Cass. I hadn't come looking for a present for Cass, but I always give her something. Back when I was immature, it was gag gifts—things that blew up or burst out of the box. Last year I gave her a key chain with a rubber sneaker on it. The fairy necklace had to be more expensive, but Cass needed cheering up. "How much is that one?" I asked.

"Which one?" The girl leaned over the glass case, her spiky purple hair darting at me like snake tongues.

"That one at the back. The fairy."

"Sweet!" She slid the door of the case open and flipped the tag. "It's eighteen."

"Eighteen dollars?" That was most of what I had for all my shopping.

"Eighteen plus tax."

If I bought it, what would I give my parents?

The girl behind the counter lifted the necklace so I could take a better look. "Want me to wrap it?" The fairy swung on her chain. "Gift wrapping's free."

I swallowed hard. "Yeah, okay." I could give Mom a coupon good for dish-washing for a month and Dad one for weeding the garden. They always say Christmas is about family, not stuff. Luckily, I already had a supersonic yo-yo for Cody. He still liked stuff.

"This must be for someone special," the girl teased.

"It's for a friend." I tried to sound offhand like Leroy, but my voice cracked.

She raised her holey eyebrows and put the fairy in a tiny white box—a jewelry box. Right then I knew I'd made a mistake. The present looked like a boy-girl gift, which it would have been if it was Leroy giving it to Jemmie. But Cass and I were friends, period.

Unless this stupid present messed the whole thing up.

chapter three

CUSTOMIZING MR. FROSTY

Monday morning, my butt had barely hit my seat when Trina Boyd passed me a note.

> *Xmas party at my house. December 23.*
> *Can you come? Pleeeeeeeze.*

I scribbled:

> *Can't. Going on vacation. Sorry.*

And I passed it back.

Trina drew a frowny face on the note and dropped it in my lap.

"Mr. Floyd." Mrs. Johnson tapped her chalk on the board. "Would you care to share that with the class?"

"No ma'am." I stuffed the note inside my science book.

Actually, I was kind of glad I couldn't go. Trina likes me. I mean *likes* me. But she says mean things about Cass all the time and makes fun of her clothes, even though she knows Cass is my friend. Any party she gave would be me, her, and a bunch of snobs.

Besides, I had more important things than Trina Boyd on my mind. Each day that passed, the Floyds were one day closer to making the big getaway. In my family, that meant doing a whole lot of work on the getaway car.

First, we had to decide which fixer-upper we would drive—Dad collects junked cars like old ladies collect stray cats. At the moment there were nine in the backyard. Five were ours. The other four belonged to guys in Dad's auto mechanics class.

"How about Mr. Frosty?" I suggested, running a hand over the side of the old ice-cream van we had begun converting to a camper. "The engine work's done."

"I don't know," he said. "I kind of wanted to slap a new paint job on her." Pictures of Fudge Blasters, Rainbow Rockets, and Dreamsicles plastered the body. The words "Mr. Frosty" were spelled out in ice-cream cones across the back doors. "Even if we forget the paint job we still have to haul the freezer out, add a seat up front, and bolt that cot to the floor." He checked the tread on a tire. "It'll take work."

"Then let's get started."

Me and Dad worked every afternoon and evening that week, starting the minute we got home. While we fixed Mr. Frosty, the neighborhood kids hung out in our yard.

Tuesday afternoon the girls got there first. Lying on her belly on the hood of a Chevy Impala, Jemmie dealt cards to Cass and Anna. Anna wore what she called her poker face, her old denim hat pulled down over her eyes. Beauty slept under the car.

Cass sat cross-legged on the fender. She didn't look all that interested in playing cards. Sometimes, when I glanced at her she was looking back. It was like she sensed the present hidden at the back of my sock drawer.

As I helped Dad horse the freezer down the ramp behind Mr. Frosty, I wondered what I'd say when I handed her the box.

Beauty lifted her head and barked once. The guys were coming around the side of the house. They were making plenty of noise, but the girls acted like they didn't hear a thing. Leroy gave one of Jemmie's braids a tug as he walked by. "Driver!" he called.

"You were driver last night," Justin complained as the guys converged on Moses Johnson's Cadillac Coupe D'Elegance. But he was already climbing in back.

Leroy folded himself in behind the wheel and hung his arm out the window. "Hey, babe!" he called to Jemmie. "Wanna go for a ride?"

Bet he had a stupid piece of jewelry in his sock drawer too.

Dad and I stood in Mr. Frosty's open back door, watching the rain fall. None of the kids had showed up, but we couldn't let a little weather stop us. It was the second-to-last night before we were set to launch. Dad nodded at our personal junkyard. "Lots of potential out there," he said, overlooking the rust and flat tires.

Dad is good at spotting potential. He sees it in guys everyone else has given up on, the ones Mr. Bodine calls delinquents. Like the cars my dad helps them fix, most of the delinquents turn out okay.

"Hey, Dad," I asked, "what are the guys going to do while you're on vacation?"

He lit a lantern and hung it from the rearview mirror. "Stay out of jail, I hope."

Weekends, and all summer long, his students hang out behind our house. They change filters, adjust belts, and see who can spit the farthest. If they're still around at mealtime Mom feeds them. Probably the only time most of them eat vegetables.

They treat me about like I treat Cody. Sometimes it's "Hey, Ben!" Other times it's "Get lost, kid." But I keep coming back. Hanging out with them I learn a lot about cars and girls. Stuff I might need later.

"There's something I've been meaning to talk to you about," Dad said, handing me a wrench. "I'll need your help on this trip."

"Help with the driving? Sure thing, Dad." He ignored that comment.

"Your mom and I are going to be real busy running the marina. Keep an extra-good eye on your brother. You know he can't swim."

"Oh, man… Is this the story of my life? What do I look like, Ben the baby-sitter?"

He punched me in the arm. "Just don't let the kid drown, okay, bud?"

"Okay." Since I had just agreed to do him a favor, I took another shot. "Now, you think I could help with the driving?"

He laughed. "As soon as you get your permit."

Dad finished tightening a bolt and stretched. His Harley Hogs T-shirt rode up. He stopped and listened to the rain drumming the metal roof. "This is pretty nice, isn't it?" he said.

"Yeah," I joked, "messing around with cars in the rain is right up there at the top of my list." But it *was* nice working with him, hearing the rain fall. It sure beat being inside with Cody and Mom, sorting laundry.

I finished tightening the last floor bolt. Dad pulled back on the seat to make sure it was secure. "Lookin' good," he said.

"Hey, Dad. We haven't packed the fishing rods." I didn't want to forget them. We have a canoe we take to Lake Talquin. Sometimes we saltwater fish off St. Marks with Dad's friend Dewey in his sixteen-foot skiff. But the way Dad told it, fishing in the Keys was killer, a whole different class.

"Run in and get 'em if you want."

"And how about the presents?"

"Tomorrow night, after your brother goes to bed," he said with a wink. "We don't want to get the presents wet, and we don't want to blow Santa's cover."

The gift for Cass was still hidden under the pile of socks. I was running out of time to give it to her. But it was late when we finished, and it was raining too hard to walk it over.

chapter four

THE DUMBEST WORDS
EVER SPOKEN

L ast night. Last chance. I dug the gift out from under my socks hoping it had changed, but it was still a little box wrapped in pink paper with silver stars on it. I found a shoe box, stuffed it with newspaper, and buried the gift in the middle. "Better," I said. I wrapped the shoe box in more newspaper—the comics.

On it I wrote:

Caution. Do not open until
December 25th...or else.

I headed for the Bodines' before I could chicken out.

I went up the walk to her door real slow. The yard was bright as day. *Blink-a-blink-a-blink.* Lights raced around every window, every door. Mr. Bodine had set up the life-size manger scene in the usual spot beside the path. A herd of plastic snowmen crowded around, admiring the plastic baby. If anyone was looking out the window they probably thought I had stopped to look at baby Jesus too. What I was really doing was putting a sneaker down on the handprints in the concrete.

Me and Cass were maybe five the day Mr. Bodine poured the path. He told us to come over and press our hands in the wet cement. While Mrs. Bodine squirted our hands with the hose, he took a stick and scratched in our names—Ben and Cassy. I don't know when I started doing it, but I step on them every time I walk the path—for luck, I guess. Tonight it was to calm myself down.

Cass's older sister, Lou Anne, answered the door. "Hi, Benji."

"Hi, Lou."

She leaned her shoulder against the door frame. Her blond hair turned green-red, green-red as the lights flashed. "I hear y'all are taking a trip."

"Yeah," I answered, "down to the Keys."

"Must be nice to go places." Lou Anne pooched out her lower lip. I shifted my weight. "Is Cass around?"

"Cass? Sure." She turned and called, "Cass? Benji's here."

I hate being called Benji. Anyone but Lou would've noticed. But Lou Anne lives in her own la-la world, like being pretty is a full-time job.

"Cass?" she hollered. "He brought you a big old present." I heard Cass's feet on the stairs. When she reached the door Lou whispered, "Told you he likes you."

Cass might've been blushing as she slid past her sister and out onto the steps. It was hard to tell with all the flashing lights.

The glass storm door closed behind her, but Lou left the inside door wide open. Her folks were probably in the kitchen. Still, I felt overexposed with that big window behind us.

Not that anything was going to happen.

Cass's green-red hair looked damp. I smelled shampoo. Everyone says Cass isn't pretty like her sister, and maybe she isn't, but Cass is someone you can spend time with. We'd been talking to each other all our lives and still hadn't run out of things to say.

Until now.

My hands were sweating all over her present. "Hi," I finally squeaked, my voice coming from the wrong side of the break.

"Want to sit?" she asked.

What I really wanted was to go back home and forget the whole thing, but I was stuck. "Yeah, okay." We'd never had to think about a dumb thing like sitting before. We bumped into each other on the way down, which had probably happened plenty of times before, only I hadn't noticed.

It was kind of cool out. Cass pulled the sleeves of her sweater down over her hands. If this was Leroy and Jemmie he'd try to put an arm around her, but we were Ben and Cass and my arms felt heavy. So we just sat there on the front stoop, the strings of lights blinking like wacko fireflies all around us. We ignored the present on my lap.

"Are you all packed and ready?" The shadow of her eyelashes fell on her cheeks.

"Yup. All set." I slid the package from my lap to the step between us.

She glanced over, but didn't touch it. She looked away, then back again. I knew curiosity would get her. A finger poked out the end of her sleeve. With it she turned the package so she could read the warning. "Or else. Or else what?"

I shrugged.

"What is it? A baseball glove?" Both hands emerged from her sleeves. She picked it up. "Too light." She gave it a shake, then looked at me. "It isn't something that'll jump out when I take the lid off, is it?"

"You'll find out on Christmas."

She punched my arm. I snatched her fist out of the air, but she pulled it away. "Is it something that'll blow up?" she asked.

"Nah, I wouldn't do that twice."

She set the package on her knees and wrapped her arms around it. "It'll be a funny kind of Christmas with you not here," she said.

I looked away. "I know."

"I've never *not* seen you on Christmas, Ben Floyd. My mom says you're part of the tradition."

"Yeah, well, I'll be thinking about you. And your mom."

She set the package on the step and jumped up. "Stay here," she said. "I have to get something."

As she went inside, the words I had just said ricocheted around in my brain. *Thinking about you?* The blinking lights must be making me crazy. *And your mom?* Had anyone ever said anything that dumb before in the whole history of the universe? If the guys heard me say a thing like that they would ride me forever. I would have to kill them to make them stop.

Cass pushed the door open with one hand. She hid the other behind her back for a second, before thrusting a flat package at me. "For you," she said. I grabbed a corner, but she wouldn't let go.

It turned into a tug of war. "You going to give this to me or not?" When she still wouldn't let go I asked, "What is it anyway?"

"It's just something," she said, still hanging on. The wrapping paper was creased like it had been used before. Even at Christmas, the Bodines don't waste a thing. "Listen, I'm giving this to you because we're friends...you know." She pushed the edge of the package into my chest and let go. "And don't open it 'til Christmas. Or else." She picked my present back up and sat, a little closer this time. We each hugged a package.

"Me and Jemmie are running in the Jingle Bell marathon," she said.

"I thought she hated marathons."

Cass nodded. "She does. She's keeping me company."

"Well, good luck."

She ran her thumbnail back and forth on the taped edge of the present. "What'll you do in the Keys?"

"I don't know. Watch the marina, pump gas, work on boats. We'll have a little time to fish and swim, I guess."

"You gonna send me a postcard?"

"A postcard? I'd be back before it got here."

"Ben..." She punched me on the leg this time. "You're going on a trip. Send me a postcard, okay?"

"Okay."

A shadow fell across us. We both jumped. Her father opened the storm door with the toe of his work boot. "Evening, Ben."

"Evening, sir." My mouth got dry watching him watch us.

I could hear the TV and Cass's little sister, Missy, crying. It was like the rest of the world had suddenly turned back on.

Mr. Bodine cleared his throat. "Well, now..." He looked as if he was trying to figure out what was going on. He had been tripping over me for the last thirteen years, but it was like he was suddenly seeing a new, dangerous Ben Floyd. "I hope you didn't spend much on that present," he said at last.

I felt like I was strangling. "No sir."

The toe of his work boot nudged the door open until the corner of the door poked me in the back. "Cass," he said. "You'd best come inside now. You're gonna catch a cold with that wet hair."

"Night, Cass," I said, standing up.

"Night, Ben." She stood and went in, but stopped just inside the door. "If I don't see you at school tomorrow, Merry Christmas. See you next year." She disappeared inside the house.

Mr. Bodine watched me leave.

I walked down the path, measuring my stride so my foot would hit the handprints in the cement. I did it casual, so Mr. Bodine wouldn't notice. But just in case he did, I took another quick look at baby Jesus before jogging back home.

chapter five

MR. FROSTY
HEADS SOUTH

I was out of my chair before the last bell quit ringing.

"Wait, Ben, wait!" Trina Boyd blocked the door.

"Sorry. Gotta go." I cut around her and tore down the hall like someone had took the lid off.

"Ben? Ben!" Trina was right behind me. "Ben!" She grabbed my shirt. "We need to talk." *She* needed to talk. All *I* needed was to get her off the back of my shirt.

She was still hanging on when I busted through the school doors.

I heard a sharp whistle and turned, swinging Trina like crack-the-whip. Mr. Frosty was parked near the buses, engine running. Dad gunned it. "Let's go, Ben. Get a move on!"

"See you, Trina. Now would ya freakin' let go?" I had to pry her fingers off me.

"Merry Christmas, Ben!" she called. I waved without looking back and dove into the van.

"We ride!" Dad shouted. He turned on the ice-cream van music. "Mary Had a Little Lamb" blared out of the loud speaker. He flicked the lights at Trina.

"Come on, Dad," I said. "Can we just go?"

"Is that Trina Boyd?" Mom hung out the window for a better look. "Isn't she the girl who keeps calling you?"

Cody had been fake-snoring on the cot, but he sat up. "Oh yeah, that's her."

"A blond," said Mom. "On the phone she sounds like a brunette. And she's cute." Mom's hair blew wildly as we picked up speed. "Don't you think she's cute, Ben?"

I tickled Cody until he collapsed on the cot gasping and Mom had lost all interest in Trina Boyd. I rested my arms on the back of Dad's seat, careful not to pull his ponytail. "Which way are we going?"

"Think we'll take Highway 27," he answered.

"Good," said Mom. "The scenic route."

"Why not the interstate?" I asked. "That old road goes through the middle of every little town in Florida. There must be a million stoplights."

"What's the rush?" Dad said. "We're on vacation."

Me and Cody lay on our bellies watching the meadows roll by through the ice-cream sales window. Cody was counting horses. "Eighteen, nineteen, twenty-one."

"You skipped twenty."

"Ben...you're so lactose intolerant." Cody was always picking things up off TV.

"Do you know what you just said?" I asked. "Lactose intolerant means that drinking milk makes me sick."

He stuck out his chin. "Not when *I* say it. When *I* say it, it means pain in the butt."

"Words don't work like that. Tell him, Mom. Tell him that lactose intolerant is wrong."

Mom twisted her hair into a bun. "Cody, use intolerant by itself," she suggested, shoving a couple of chopsticks through the knot of hair. "That would be correct."

I fell back on the cot. "Thanks for your support, Mom."

But once Cody latches onto something, he keeps it up. I was lactose intolerant when I wouldn't let him unlock the men's room with the big key.

And *so* lactose intolerant when we stopped for supper and got into an argument about whether or not he could swim. "I can too swim," he said, hiding a forkful of peas under his napkin.

"Can not." I lifted the napkin so Mom could see.

"Can too. I float in the tub." He slid a few peas off his plate and let them fall on the floor. "You are *so* lactose intolerant!"

Dad's fork clattered onto his plate. "Enough," he said. "Do you boys realize where you're going?"

But Cody was still revved. "Hey, Ben, like seafood?" he hissed, then stuck out his tongue at me. There were bits of carrot all over it. "Get it? *See* food!"

"Nice, Cody. Real nice." I rolled my eyes toward Dad.

But Dad put one hand on each of our heads and pressed down. "Do I have your full attention?" he asked. Then he nodded our heads for us. "Good. Because I am going to tell you boys about Bert's Marina and you will feel so lucky, you will get along like peas and carrots for the whole rest of the trip." I bet he used the word "peas" to let Cody know he'd seen the disappearing pea trick.

Dad leaned back in the booth. "Where to begin?" he said. He cracked his knuckles thoughtfully, one by one. Mom gave him the look she gives him every time he does that, but he was focused on the story—no, the legend—of Bert's Marina.

"Every summer, when I was a kid, my folks would send me to stay with Uncle Bert and Aunt Emma," he started. "I was scared the first summer. I missed my parents and the kids back home. My cousins could do anything, especially Bob, who was two months younger than me. He could swim like a fish, haul lobster traps, sandball for yellowtail. About all I could do was ride a bike." He put a hand next to his mouth and whispered, "Don't tell your mother, but I was a wimp."

"No!" Cody protested.

"Believe it, Cody. But Bert's Marina de-wimped me. By the time my folks picked me up I could catch and clean a fish and do back-flips off the pilings. I could dive twelve feet down and get a seashell off the bottom." We'd heard Dad's marina stories all our lives. Usually we were like, yeah, yeah. But this time we listened.

Cody leaned on his elbows. "You forgot to tell about Slip."

"Good old Slip-In-Easy." Dad shook his head, remembering. "I fed him every morning, and you boys can too."

I was ready to move right into my father's story—hang out with cousin Bob, fish, and feed Slip. But cousin Bob was grown up now, working in Orlando. And how long can a heron live, anyway? "Come on, Dad, Slip's a pile of bones by now."

"Son of Slip then, or great-great grandson of Slip. There's always a heron named Slip-In-Easy at your uncle's marina."

And always guys hanging around the marina. I remembered that part of the story. Houseboats, cruisers, and sailboats all tied up at Uncle Bert's dock, every one of them a live-aboard that added kids to the mix of cousins. It didn't matter if Slip was a different Slip and the kids were different kids. This would be *my* Bert's Marina, not Dad's. I'd have a few stories of my own to tell.

"So how about if you boys call a truce?" Dad was saying. "We have an all-night haul ahead of us."

"My offer to help drive is still good."

He slapped me on the shoulder. "Thanks, bud. I can handle it." He dropped a generous tip on the table. "What do you say, amigos?"

"We ride!" Cody shouted.

My brother fell asleep as soon as the sun went down. A while later I did too, but I kept waking up with his elbow in my ear or his arm across my neck. Dad turned on the radio we'd installed. He and Mom sang along. Oldie goldies.

The next time we stopped, I woke up just long enough to hear Dad say, "Think I'd better kick back a couple of hours." While he slept in his seat, Mom sat on a rest-stop picnic table and watched the stars. She doesn't drive a stick shift. As I went back to sleep I wished I was older or the driving age was younger. I can handle a stick.

I woke up again when Dad pulled into a diner. Cody was spread out like a starfish. I pulled my leg out from under his, then hobbled around the parking lot, trying to bring my foot back to life. I sat down on the curb, folded my hands behind my head, and lay back in the grass. The fronds of the palms in front of the diner clattered in the warm breeze, a sound I didn't hear at home.

As I looked up into the dark, starry sky, I felt like I was expanding. The neighborhood and the kids I spent every single day with seemed as small and far away as the stars.

chapter six

WELCOME TO BERT'S MARINA

Dad bellowed, "Rise and shine, boys!" When I opened my eyes, I was scrunched against the back of Cody's shirt, breathing the smell of stale brother. "We there?" I asked, sitting up.

"Yup." Dad cut the engine and hung his arms over the wheel. "Welcome to Bert's Marina, boys!"

Cody sat up and rubbed his eyes. "Where's Slip?" All we could see through the ice-cream window was a cloud of dust.

Cody stared, blinked, then stared some more. The dust was settling. "This is it?"

"Great, isn't it?" Dad jumped from the truck and spread his arms as if he wanted to bear-hug the whole place. "It's exactly the way I remember it."

"It *is?*" said Cody. *"Exactly?"*

Through the window we could see a dumpy blue building with a sign in the window that blinked Chum-Bait-Ice, Chum-Bait-Ice. "Just like home," Cody whispered. He pointed toward the broken-down powerboats waiting to be fixed. "Except with dead boats instead of dead cars." He read some of the names painted on them. "Joe's Paycheck, Lucky Linda. Best Re... Best Rev..."

"Revenge, Cody." The four-wheeled trailer under *Best Revenge* had three flats. I elbowed my brother and whispered, "Looks like Dad-heaven, doesn't it?"

"Dad-heaven," he echoed.

Cody was disappointed, but I wasn't. I was somewhere that was not-home. *Really* not-home. I'd remembered right about the daylight. The sun was barely up but it about peeled the backs off my eyes. Bushes covered with hot pink flowers smothered up against the blue walls of the store. Under one bush lay a heap of cannonballs. Leaning next to the door was a huge rusted anchor that was taller than the building. "Hey, Dad, what's the story on the anchor?" I asked.

"Uncle Bert brought it up from the bottom. It came off a Spanish galleon."

"You hear that?" I squeezed Cody's arm. "A Spanish galleon!" I listened for the sounds of kids, but it was still pretty early. They'd probably been up late, night-fishing.

"What do you say, Floyds?" Dad boomed. "You gonna spend your whole vacation in the truck?" He slid open the passenger door, grabbed Mom by the waist, and swung her out of her seat. Her skirt fluttered. Some time in the night she'd taken off her Tallahassee shoes. The first thing she did when her bare feet touched down was pull the chopsticks out of her bun and shake her head. Her loose hair spilled around her shoulders. She picked a floppy red flower off a bush next to the anchor and tucked it behind one ear.

"Welcome to the islands," she said.

Dad did the red flower thing too. "Let the adventure begin!" he proclaimed.

When we climbed out, Mom tried to stick a flower behind Cody's ear. *"Mom!"* he wailed. "Do I look like a girl to you?"

"Cody!" she mimicked, tucking the flower behind her other ear. "You are *so* lactose intolerant!"

Dad lifted a cannonball and picked up a key. The door opened with a moan. We all rushed into the cool dark of the dockside store. It smelled good in there, like motor oil and rust. Shelves of fishing tackle and junk food and Styrofoam coolers stood in the middle of the room, but against the walls were cardboard boxes, stacked and slumping. "I see Uncle Bert still hangs onto everything," Dad said, poking a box with his toe.

"What's in them?" Cody asked.

"Parts," said Dad. "Important parts." Then he laughed. "Too bad most are for engines they don't make any more. But then, your uncle couldn't find the one he needed if his life depended on it."

Mom picked up the long note Aunt Emma had left on the counter. "What to do if the pump on the shrimp tank clogs," she read.

Dad flipped the Gone Fishin' sign around in the window. "Bert's Marina is under new management," he said. "And we are open for business!"

Mom grabbed the envelope with the houseboat key inside. "*You* may be open," she said. "The boys and I are going to check out the accommodations."

"Yeah," I said. "Cody never slept on a houseboat before." I acted like some old hand because I'd slept aboard when I was four, but I was excited too. Who wouldn't be excited about living on a boat?

My brother and I lay on the warm boards of the dock, chins on our arms. "What're those?" Cody asked. Some small fish with black and yellow stripes were nibbling the weeds at the base of a piling.

"How would I know?" I turned my head and gazed at the long, empty stretch of dock between us and the store. "Do you think we're the only ones here?"

"Looks like it," said Cody.

"Let's get some drinks," I suggested, still hoping the other boats were out for the day.

When we got to the store, Dad was digging through one of Uncle Bert's toolboxes. "Hey, Dad?" I said. "Where are all the live-aboards? Looks like Uncle Bert's houseboat's the only one."

"Regulations have gotten mighty tight in the last few years. Uncle Bert didn't want to have to build a big restroom with showers and all.

He still lets an occasional live-aboard tie up if the people use the shower and restroom in the shop." He turned to Mom. "Emma's note mentioned someone coming by in the next day or two, didn't it?"

Mom stood barefoot on the cool concrete floor, skimming Aunt Emma's note. "A man with one child," she said.

"Is the child a guy, mom?"

"It just says child." She pushed a button on the register. The cash drawer popped open with a *ding*. "I've always wanted to do that," she said. Cody had to try it too.

While Cody punched keys, I thought about the word "child." Cody was a child. I was a guy. But Aunt Emma was pretty old. Maybe to her anyone under, say, fifteen was a child.

By the second time we walked past the empty slips on our way to the store, I was imagining a boat parked behind the houseboat. A father and a guy.

"Look at all these hooks!" Mom shuddered, contemplating a display of lures. "There has to be a kinder way. Sometimes I think—"

I put my arm around her neck. "You think too much. Give it a rest, Mom." I walked to the back of the shop and smacked the screen door open. Maybe I could help Dad with something.

Dad was under the awning in my uncle's outdoor boat repair shop. You would think that after driving all night, he would want to crash. Instead he had taken the engine cover off the *Lucky Linda* and pulled the plugs. "Want some help?" I asked. *Pleeeeeease...*I added silently.

He lifted his baseball cap and wiped his face. "Nah, you boys hang out."

So it was back to lying on the dock. "The striped ones are called sergeant majors," I said, pointing to a drawing on the fish ID card we'd borrowed off a rack in the store.

"Sergeant majors, sergeant majors," Cody repeated.

After watching the fish a while, my brother turned his head on his arms and looked at the last live-aboard. "It's just like a floating house, isn't it, Ben?" A hand-painted sign that said Bert 'N Emma's Loveboat was nailed above its door.

Flower baskets hung from the *Loveboat's* roof. My aunt had covered the front door with shiny paper and taped a big wide ribbon up so the door looked like a Christmas present. But with the hot sun beating on our backs it didn't feel like Christmas.

"Look," Cody said. "They have a rocking chair just like Cass's."

"Hey, you're right." Cass shares a room with her sister, so she keeps a chair hidden behind a bush in the yard. It's all sun-bleached and creaky, but she sits back there when she wants to get away from her family.

I was imagining Cass in her chair when I heard the blast of a horn. We lifted our heads. A cabin cruiser out on Snake Creek had pulled even with the end of the canal. The bridge tender answered with a horn blast of his own. There was a *clang, clang, clang,* and traffic stopped. "Whoa!" said Cody as the middle of the bridge lifted eighty feet in the air. He waved at the boat that passed through, making its way to the Atlantic.

Bert's Marina is on a deep-water canal off Snake Creek, which isn't a creek at all, but a passage between Windley Key and Plantation Key. "Key" is what they call an island down here. At one end of the creek is Florida Bay, at the other is the Atlantic. The steady boat traffic between the two keeps my uncle in business.

In the couple of hours Cody and I lazed around the dock, eight boats turned into the canal to fuel up. Each time, Mom dashed down the wooden steps to the gas dock. "Need help? Can I get you bait or ice or anything?" She would have looked like she'd been there all her life—except she was as white as a peeled potato. I heard Dad call to her, "Slow down, Samantha Jean. Kick back. You're on Keys'-time now."

As the sleek powerboats came and went it got hotter. In a while, the dock wasn't so comfortable to lie on anymore. "Let's go swimming," Cody said, jumping up.

"Better get some water wings. You don't know how to swim, remember?"

"Do too!"

"Do not!"

He scampered down the dock and jumped aboard the houseboat, then pinwheeled his arms to keep his balance as the boat rocked.

Still arguing over whether or not he could swim, we raced to our cabin. As I dug for trunks in my suitcase, I saw a little corner of Cass's gift. It made me think of my present for her, ticking away like a time bomb until she opened it. I jammed a T-shirt down over the crinkled paper and got my trunks out.

"No looking," Cody said.

"At what?" I asked, but we put our swimsuits on facing away.

"Oh, this is bad," I said when the two of us turned around.

Cody gave himself hiccups. "We look like we have the wrong heads!" he gulped, laughing at the two boys in Aunt Emma's full-length mirror. Except for tan faces and the lower parts of our arms, we were both pure white.

"School sure sucked the color out of us," I said.

"Race ya!" My brother ran for the door. "I'm jumping in first!"

"But you can't swim!" I shouted, chasing his skinny butt. I snatched at the elastic waist of his trunks, but missed. When we hit the dock I grabbed his arm before he could launch and lowered him on the shallow side where the water was only ankle deep.

He had barely touched down when he started dancing around, yelling, "Gross, Ben! There's all these crunchy things!" Cody's used to Wakulla Springs, where the bottom is pure sand. This canal had stuff growing in it—little fan-like green things, and brushy green things, and segmented things the color of celery. He let out a high-pitched scream.

"Oh, quit being such a girl." I sat on the dock and dropped into the water. A bunch of gritty stuff squeezed up between my toes. "Let's get out a little deeper." We crawled under the dock, crunching more things with our knees.

When we stood up again, the water was waist deep on me, the bottom falling away fast. "Cody, run up to the store and get those water wings."

"Look at this." Light ribboned up Cody's arm as he swished it around underwater.

"Nice. Now go get those wings."

He floated his hand up to the surface and made a fist. A geyser shot up. "Cool. Hey, look at the fish by my feet, Ben!" Then he let out another screech and kicked. "They're biting!"

"Those're minnows, for Pete's sake. They hardly have mouths." Speckled fish the color of sand were nibbling my feet too, but I was more concerned about the way the bottom dropped off. It was there—the water was so clear you could see every grain of sand—and then it was gone. The canal had been dynamited out of the coral bedrock of the island. According to Dad, it was twenty-two feet deep. "Get those water wings, *now.*"

"Wait, I'll show ya I can swim." In one sloppy stroke he left the safe, shallow edge of the canal. He arched his back, holding his head up like a swimming dog. For a second I thought, Wow, maybe he *can* swim.

Then he went under. Bubbles blubbed out of his mouth. There was no sound, but I knew he was shouting, "Ben!" That's what Cody shouts anytime he gets in trouble.

He popped up for a second, "Be—" He didn't even get the *n* out before he was under again. I saw his blue eyes open and close as he sank.

I thrashed after him, grabbed him by the trunks, and hauled him back. I felt for the bottom with my toes, but couldn't find it.

"What're you trying to do?" he sputtered as I jammed my feet into the crunchy sand. "De-pants me?"

"What're *you* trying to do, drown?" I shoved him up on the dock. "Get water wings like I told you to in the first place." He trotted off, trunks dripping.

I watched him until the screen door slammed behind him. Great, I thought. All this water and a kid brother who can't swim. I'll be on constant Cody-patrol.

I swam out over the deep part of the canal, working on my crawl. My family only hits Wakulla Springs a couple times a summer, Cape San Blas maybe once. I'm a pretty decent swimmer considering how little practice I get. If I didn't have Cody to watch, I could be a lot better by the end of the vacation.

Cody trotted down the dock wearing a pair of orange balloons on his arms. He was dragging a towel. "Got my wings. See?" His arms stuck out from his sides and he was slathered all over with white cream. "Mom says for you to grease up too. She says to dry off first so it'll stick." I climbed out, dried off, greased up, and got back in.

"I gotcha, Cody." I reached up to lift him down, but he jumped. *Splash!* With the wings on, he bobbed right back up.

"See?" he said. "Told ya I could swim." And he frogged away, headed straight out.

"Far enough," I called. "Now come on back."

He kept kicking.

"You want me to tie a rope to you?"

Splash, splash, splash. Pretty soon he'd be crawling up on the boat ramp at the Coast Guard station on the other side, putting in a surprise appearance.

I almost shouted something to him about sharks. That would definitely get him back. Cody wouldn't even go near a bathtub for a couple of weeks after watching *Jaws* at Justin's house. But if I got him all scared, he'd show up in my bed in the middle of the night. Instead, I warned, "I'm counting, Cody. You better be back here by five."

chapter seven

MICA

We were splashing around in the middle of the canal when the next boat signaled the bridge. The blast came from the ocean side so I couldn't see the boat. While the other horns had sounded big and bossy, this one sounded weak, like it was begging to be let in. Still, I didn't want to take a chance on getting plowed under if the boat turned into the canal. "Head for the dock, Cody. Now."

It turned out we had plenty of time. Bells clanged, the bridge lifted. For a long while nothing came through. What finally nosed through the opening was an old sailboat. Dull maroon, it looked like a shoe someone had worn until it was scuffed all over. Its lumpy sails were bound. Its engine coughed. The hull shuddered as it turned into our canal.

It was still wallowing in the turn when a skinny girl in a blue swimsuit with a white stripe down each side dashed out onto the narrow piece of wood that stuck out of the sailboat's bow. She looked about ten, eleven at the most. Her wild hair blew back like a mane.

"She's gonna fall in," Cody predicted. I thought she would too, since the only thing she held onto was the big pink seashell she'd blown to signal the bridge.

She thrust out the hand with the shell in it. "A little to starboard," she called. The boat corrected course.

If she falls, the boat'll go right over her, I thought as the sailboat overcorrected.

Out went the other arm. "A little to port now, Captain." The girl was real tan.

I looked down at my pasty chest. I bent my knees until only my head was above water.

"Hey, girl on the boat! Hi!" Cody kicked away from the dock. He waved so hard that, even with the wings on, he dunked himself. He came up coughing but went right on yelling, "Over here! My name's Cody. This is Ben. We're brothers."

The girl turned and squinted at the water. "Hi, brothers!" She waved the shell.

Now Cody would swim over to the pumps and have a big old conversation with the girl. When she left he'd splash after her yelling, "Bye, girl on the boat, bye," and wave until the sailboat disappeared.

But the sailboat never made it to the gas pumps. Instead, it docked in the empty slip right behind the houseboat. *No. This can't be happening.* The captain cut the engine.

"Got it." The girl grabbed a line and leapt to the dock as easy as a cat. Her bony knees stuck out as she lashed the bowline to a cleat. She hurried to the stern and caught the rope the man threw to her. She tied it quick, as if the sailboat might get away. But that old boat practically leaned against the pilings. Maybe this is an emergency stop, I thought. Something's broke. Dad'll fix it, and they'll sail away.

Cody was trying to sound out the sailboat's name. "Mmmm...arrr..."

"Martina," I whispered. Maybe that was the girl's name, Martina. But the lettering looked faded, like it was painted on the boat before she was even born.

She shook her bangs out of her eyes. "All secure, Captain."

The man lifted his pith helmet and ran a hand through his hair. He was dressed like he was on safari. His khaki shorts and shirt had pockets all over them. Manning the wheel, he had stood very straight, but he walked with a limp. He had a hard time lowering himself to the dock, even with one hand on the girl's shoulder. He gave her one quick pat on the head, then lurched away.

The girl twined her arms around herself and watched him walk slowly down the dock. If he needed bait or ice or something, he should have sent her.

When he made it to the store he rested against the railing before tackling the four stairs to the back deck.

"Hi, girl!" Cody burst out. I smacked him on the back to shut him up, but he just yelled again. "Hey, over here!"

The girl turned, still hugging herself, and strolled over. Before she reached our part of the dock, she did a cartwheel. "Hi, brothers." She plopped down on the dock and swung her legs, dragging her big toes in the water. In the middle of each toenail was a chip of red polish. "What's up?" she asked.

"We're swimming!" Cody got her all wet showing off his kick, but she didn't seem impressed.

"That's not *really* swimming," she said. "Take those baby water wings off."

"He's not taking them off," I said. "Cody, you're not taking them off."

"Is your big brother always this bossy?" the girl asked.

"Yup. Ben is completely lactose intolerant."

She stared at my face. "Is that why he has zits?"

What zits? I thought. I don't have zits. Justin's the one with zits. I wished he was here for comparison. I wished he was here, period.

Cody grabbed the girl's ankles and gazed up at her. "What's your name?" he asked.

She swung her legs, swishing him through the water. "Mica."

"You're named after a rock?" I said.

"Not just any old rock." She leaned back on her arms. "Mica is a glittering rock of crystalline construction, ranging in color from canary yellow to palest gray."

"A rock's a rock," I said.

"I'm seven minus two months," said Cody. "How old are you?"

"Eleven," said Mica. She had Bugs Bunny front teeth, like she was still growing into them. "And how old is brother Ben?"

"Thirteen and a half," I said.

"Really." She wrinkled her peeling nose. "Thirteen and a *whole* half?"

I should've rounded up.

Cody pointed to the chain that hung around her neck. "What's that ring for? Why don't you put it on your finger?"

The girl held out the chain and the gold ring on it spun. "It's my mother's wedding ring. She asked me to keep it until she gets back."

"Back from where?" Cody wondered.

"The continent."

"Which continent?" I asked. "There are seven."

"Europe, of course." She flipped a little water at me with one toe. "She's on tour. My mother is the famous ballet dancer, Martina Montero." She looked at us, like the name should set off fireworks.

I crossed my arms. "Never heard of her."

"Your mother went off and left you?" Cody breathed. He was still at the stage where he told Mom that he was never going to leave her and Dad, ever. He planned to keep his same room, even when he went to college.

The girl shrugged. "She had to go. She's a dancer."

The back door of the marina store opened. Our mother and the man stepped onto the deck. They stood beside the bubbling shrimp tank, talking. I noticed he was empty-handed. Maybe he wanted to buy live shrimp for bait. If I knew Mom, she was trying to talk him out of it. She hated the idea of sticking a hook in a live animal.

"That's *my* mother," Cody blurted out. "She likes to dance too, but mostly she's a mom. Oh, she also works at the utility company."

Mom stood at the top of the stairs. Her brown hair looked reddish in the light. "Your mother's so pretty," Mica said.

"Beautiful," Cody agreed.

"That's my father. *Dr.* Robin Michael Delano, the famous marine biologist. He's one of the world's foremost authorities on the benthic community."

Cody blinked. "The what-ick community?"

"*Ben*-thic. The benthic community is everything that lives on, or just under, the ocean floor." She spoke slowly, like she was trying to teach a dog how to sit. "This includes the plants, the animals, the microorganisms. Everything."

The benthic specialist waved a hand at Mica. She hopped up and sprinted over to him.

"What's going on?" Cody asked. "He's introducing her to Mom." As Mom shook Mica's hand, I got a sinking feeling. It seemed awfully elaborate if all they wanted to do was buy bait. And if they needed a repair, Dad would be talking to them.

Mica and her father walked back slowly. "Where are Uncle Bert and Aunt Emma?" I heard her ask. While he explained about the cruise, I wondered if the little know-it-all was some long-lost cousin.

When Dr. Delano's beat-up hiking boots and Mica's bare feet stopped, they were standing on the dock beside me and Cody. "Captain, see those boys in the water?" A big toe with a chip of red polish in the middle pointed at us. "They're my new friends, Cody and Ben."

Friends? Stunned, I looked up at Dr. Delano. What was she talking about?

"Friends already?" He raised his eyebrows. "This is a new speed record, even for you."

He dug a small key out of a pocket. "Does this look familiar?" he asked. "The key to the bathhouse?" By that he probably meant the shower at the back of the store. He lifted the chain from around her neck, undid the catch, and threaded the small key on it. "This time don't lose it."

She made a face as the chain dropped back over her head. "I won't, sir."

There went my last hope. Mica and her dad were the man and

child my aunt had mentioned in her note. Turned out, the "child" part was accurate.

"Let's see, now." Dr. Delano drummed his fingers on his chin. "What do we have to work with?" Mica stroked the top of his boot with her foot, but he didn't seem to notice. "Say, that wasn't here last year." The boots lurched over to a picnic table that sat on an extension of the pier just behind their sailboat. The bare feet looked stranded. "This should do nicely," he said. "All we need to do is rig a little shade for the tanks."

"Tanks?" Cody jumped up and down in the water. "Tanks of what?"

"Aquariums." Mica dropped to a squat. "For our specimens, of course."

"Me and Ben'll help, won't we, Ben?" Cody scrambled under the dock and got out on the shallow side. I scorched my palms boosting myself up on the dock. I didn't want to crawl under in front of Mica.

The dock was too hot for standing around on. Cody picked up one foot, then the other. Each time, he pressed his arch against the inside of the opposite knee. Mom called it "doing a flamingo." I was tempted to do one too, but figured we already looked dumb enough with our trunks glued to our legs and our pale chests sticking out.

The hot dock didn't seem to bother Mica, though. Her feet were brown and tough, like ours in the summer. "Don't just stand there," she said. "We have stuff to unload." She reached for a post and swung herself up onto the deck of the *Martina,* then tapped one tough bare foot. "Come on, Ben, grab a stanchion." I grabbed the post and stepped up.

Cody tried to climb aboard too.

"Stay there," I told him. "We'll pass you stuff."

Mica lifted a hatch cover. Butt in the air, she reached in and grabbed something. "Here's the tarp."

I dumped the armload of blue plastic on Cody. He dragged it over to the picnic table. Next came a hammer, nails, and wood. .

Dr. Delano hit his finger nailing up posts. Nana Grace would never let *him* hammer pecans, not if she heard the words he spouted.

The Delanos stretched out the tarp and held it up. I drove nails through the grommets and into the posts. I had to wipe sweat out of my eyes a couple of times, but I drove every single nail nice and straight. When we were done, there was a patch of cool, blue shade under the tarp. Cody scrambled up on the table and sat. I had just parked my butt too when Mica grabbed my arm.

"Quit resting on your laurels," she said, dragging me back aboard the *Martina*. "You stay topside," she ordered. "I'll hand the aquariums up the companionway." As she passed tanks up the ladder I tried to look inside the boat, but all I could see was a wooden floor and a shelf of books. The boat looked dark and kind of bare.

Stowed inside the aquariums were pumps and tubing and the thick outdoor power cord that everything would plug into. Cody dumped them all in a heap.

After Dr. Delano and I straightened out my brother's mess, I helped him set up the aquariums. He had to tell me what to do, but he seemed to appreciate the help. Dr. Delano was probably as young as my parents, but he moved old. He reminded me of Anna's patched-up dog, Beauty. His bad leg had scars all over it. The left side of his face looked scraped. Healed in under the skin were dark spots, like some of what had hurt him had been left behind.

I didn't realize I was staring until Mica hissed, "Motorcycle accident. Tell your brother to quit staring too."

I whapped Cody on the arm. He stopped.

I helped Dr. Delano lower a moped from the deck of the *Martina*. "Thank you, son." I guess he had already forgotten my name. "Mica and I always have trouble with that." He gave a stiff nod. I nodded back.

To fill the aquariums, we hauled water in a bucket dropped over the far side of the sailboat. "The water at the edge of the canal has too much sediment in it," Mica explained.

Mica was emptying the bucket into one of the tanks when a white bird with a black head swooped low over the dock. Dr. Delano pointed and said, "Identify."

"Easy cheesy," Mica said. "Laughing gull, *Larus atricilla.* Common in summer along the Atlantic and Gulf coasts." While reciting from memory, she did a handstand. "They've declined in recent years due to habitat destruction."

I didn't know if we were supposed to be impressed or if it was a game the two of them played, like Dad and me naming the make and model of cars as they drove by. While she rattled off her answer, the benthic expert kept on laying out the power cord. When it was clear she thought she was done he shot her a sneaky look. "Similar species?"

"Franklin's gull," she sang, doing a cartwheel like she was home free.

"Good, good." He glanced at her again. "There is another one, you know."

Mica had her arms stretched over her head, her toe pointed for a second cartwheel. "Another one?"

"Yes, indeed." He flipped the cover over the outlet on the piling and plugged the cord in. Pumps hummed. Bubbles wiggled up from the bottom of each tank. Dr. Delano turned to his daughter. "Bonaparte's gull." He licked his finger and drew a line in the air. "Score one for the old man."

A little while later, a second bird flew overhead, a gray one this time. She sat up straight, eager to recite. But by then her father was messing with one of the pumps. He seemed to have forgotten the game.

The unnamed bird flew over the bridge and out to sea.

chapter eight

ISLAND COLLECTING

Mica curled her toes around the ends of the bleached boards of the dock. "He runs a marine biology fun camp at Caloosa Lodge," she said as her father walked away. "He has to check in. It starts tomorrow."

"How long does it last?" I asked, hoping it was just a couple of days.

She held her hair up off her neck. "All season." I didn't know what season she was talking about, but it had to be longer than a week.

"Fun camp?" Cody repeated, watching Dr. Delano lift the receiver on the pay phone in front of the store. "Can we go?"

"Forget it, Cody." Mica let her hair fall around her shoulders. "Trust me, it's not so fun. When he taught there last year, I had to go every single day. No one really wanted to learn about biology. The camp is just so rich people on vacation can get rid of their kids." She shaded her eyes and watched her dad. "He hates it too. He's only doing it because he's between research grants right now." She spun and faced us again, eyes lit. "Hey, I have an idea! I can stay here and hang out with you guys! What do you say?"

"Great!" Cody slapped his hands together. "Right, Ben?"

"Yeah...great." Was I doomed? Any time anything the least bit cool was about to happen to me somebody said, "Fine, but could you keep an eye on your brother?" Now I'd be baby-sitting two kids instead of one. My big vacation began to fold up small.

"Both of you, take off anything shiny," Mica commanded. She lifted the chain from around her neck and dropped it over a piling.

"How come?" Cody asked, even though all he had on was a pair of wet swim trunks and the orange balloons on his arms.

"Barracudas. Shiny things attract them. Now, watch this, guys!" And she hopped aboard the *Martina*. I thought she was going to jump over the side, make a big splash. Instead she climbed up the rigging to the very top of the mast.

Cody tipped his head way back. "What's she doing up there?"

"How should I know?"

Mica stood on a small bar. She grabbed the mast with one hand and leaned way out. "Dare me to jump?" she yelled.

"Go ahead," I yelled back. "Knock yourself out."

She was stepping around to the other side of the mast when her foot slipped. My heart punched the inside of my chest. Cody screamed.

"Ha, ha!" she called down. "Just kidding!" Her feet were still on the same little bar, but now the mast was behind her. She reached back, grabbed it, then leaned out over the water. In a moment she pulled in again.

She raised up on her toes slowly and lifted her arms over her head. "You guys watching? Here goes!" Suddenly, she was in the air. Head down, toes and fingers pointed, she looked like a falling knife.

The water closed over her as smooth as a sheet of glass. Cody was barely breathing.

"Show off," I said. If she expected me to clap when she came up, it wasn't going to happen. Only problem was, she didn't come up. All that came up were a few bubbles…

A few more bubbles…and then…

Nothing.

"Dive in, Ben. You gotta save her!" Cody gave me a shove.

"I didn't tell her to jump." I scraped my knee climbing aboard the *Martina*. I looked over the side, killing time, expecting her to pop back up any second.

"Maybe a bac-a-ruda got her!" Cody screamed. "Maybe her head's stuck in the mud!"

Arms spread for balance, I wobbled out to the end of the skinny board—it was like walking the plank. As the boat rose and fell, I remembered her standing out there guiding the boat into the canal.

Cody was going nuts. "Maybe she's drownding. Dive down, Ben. Save her!"

Mom says I'm my brother's hero. She teases me about having a big Superman *S* on my chest only Cody can see.

"Ben?" His shrill little voice jabbed at me. "Ben? What are you waiting for?"

I hit the water hard. Bubbles blasted by my ears, making sharp, crackling sounds. I hadn't been but five or six feet above the water when I jumped, but I seemed to be going awful deep. I tried to force my eyelids open, but they were on strike.

I came up spewing saltwater, gasping…

"You brothers really can't swim, can you?" said a taunting voice.

I opened my eyes, and there was Mica doing a lazy backstroke in a circle around me.

"Ben can swim," Cody said, sticking up for me. "He swims good. Me too." Then he held his nose and jumped.

Mica disappeared on one side of me, then popped up again on the other. "Want to dive off my mast, brother Ben?"

"Think I'll pass. I get nosebleeds," I joked. The truth is, I have a problem with heights. I wasn't about to work on it in front of Mica.

Cody splashed around beside the dock. "See? Told ya I could swim."

Mica paddled over and hung onto one of the *Martina*'s mooring ropes. Cody latched on next to her. "You coming?" he called. I swam over and got on his other side. We all hung there with the rope under our armpits.

"See those little striped fish under the dock?" Cody said. "They're called sergeant majors."

"Latin name, *Abudefduf saxatilis,*" said Mica.

"What do you mean, Latin name?" Cody waved his foot, trying to spook the fish. "Is Latin some kind of secret language?"

"All the animals ever discovered have a regular name and a Latin name," she said. "The Latin name is what scientists, like me and the Captain, call them."

"I hate to break this to you," I told the punky girl hanging on the rope on the other side of Cody, "but you're not a scientist. You're a kid."

"I am too a scientist! Ask the Captain. I help him all the time."

"Like you help Dad with cars," my brother said.

"That doesn't make me a mechanic."

Showing off how scientific she was, Mica started telling Cody all about sergeant majors. "They feed on plankton, invertebrates, sometimes even plants. They're way bigger in the islands, as big as your hand."

The Continent, I thought. *The* Islands. Mica reminded me of the girls at school who stop whispering to each other the minute a guy walks up. I had them figured out. If I want them to tell me what they're whispering about, all I have to do is keep my mouth shut and one of them'll say, "Want to tell Ben? I think we should." When they do tell, it's usually something stupid. Like Mica's islands. *The* Islands.

"Grand Bahama, Eleuthera, Martinique…" Mica recited island names like each was a link in a long sparkling chain. "My father and I island-hop all the time. Islands are my hobby. I collect them."

"I collect bottle caps," Cody said. "Ben collects stamps. You have some of islands, don't you, Ben?"

"Yeah," I said, swinging my legs in the water. "That's how I collect islands. They're easier to put in the book."

"Bo-ring." Mica did a front roll over the rope.

"What about school?" Cody asked.

She shook water out of her eyes. "What about it?"

"How do you go to school if you're sailing around all the time collecting islands?"

"I don't." Mica did another roll and came up with her hair slicked back. "School comes to me. Want to somersault, Cody? Just take a few deep breaths, then go for it."

"Hold the phone," I said. "How do you do that?"

"Do what?" she asked as Cody hyperventilated. "Take a deep breath?"

"Yeah, I've been wondering how to do that." She made me want to drop the whole thing, but I was curious. "You know... How do you get school to come to you?"

"Easy cheesy. You take a couple tests, send some money, and once a month you get a package of assignments. When the work is done you mail it back." She slapped a hand over my brother's mouth. "All right, Cody! Quit puffing. You'll make yourself dizzy." She tried to shove him over the rope but the water wings popped him back up.

"You mean you never go to a real school?" I pressed.

"Like, sit at a desk?" She put a hand under Cody's butt and shoved. "No way. I do my schoolwork at the beach or on the boat. It takes about three hours a day." She grabbed Cody by the hair and pulled him back up. "Take those stupid water wings off. Now."

"Leave 'em on," I said. "What do you mean, three hours a day?"

"Sixty minutes times three." Mica pulled the plug on the wing that was on her side. "I'm super-smart so I learn fast. I don't have to wait around for the dummies to catch on." She hugged the plastic wing, squeezing the air out.

"Stop that." I tried to pry her arms off Cody, but she hung on.

"He'll be okay," she said as the little stream of air hit me on the neck. "You get the other one." When I wouldn't do it, she reached around and tried to pull the plug herself.

I shoved her hand away. "All right," I said. "But we have to stay with him." I popped the plug and started squeezing air out. "How come I've never heard of going to school by mail?"

"Like you've heard of everything?" She peeled the withered wing off Cody's arm and tossed it on the dock. "For your information, all kinds of kids go to school by mail."

"What kinds?" I asked.

"Live-aboard kids, like me, and kids who work for circuses and carnivals. Sick kids."

Just three hours a day, I thought, forcing the last of the air out. No sitting still all day wishing I was outdoors. No watching the black hands of the clock creep. There had to be a hitch. "Do you like it?"

"Are you kidding? It's outstanding! I have lots of time to swim and dive and sail. I can help my dad do science."

Great. There's no hitch. While I'm a prisoner of Monroe Middle, she's out sailing around collecting islands. I hurled the second wing onto the dock.

"Mica…" Cody tugged on her arm. "Show me the trick."

"What's there to show?" I said, and I shoved him over the rope.

He came up coughing.

Mica glared. "You should've told him to blow air out his nose."

Cody glared too, like I purposely hadn't told him, then turned to Mica. "What do I do?"

"Blow out through your nose. Gently. You want to try again?"

He coughed one more time in my direction, then nodded.

When Mica Delano got done with my brother he still didn't know how to swim, but she had him rolling over that rope like a performing dolphin.

After that, the two of them sat huddled on the crunchy side of the dock, speaking Latin. It turned out that all the little brushy, segmented, gritty things had names—Latin and English. Cody parroted each one. Lactose intolerant was about to be replaced.

Maybe I am too, I thought as I paddled around. Fine. Let her be his hero a while. This one needed a break.

chapter nine

SLIP-IN-EASY

White lines twisted like snakes across the ceiling above my bunk. It took a while to figure out it was just sunlight reflected off the ripples in the canal. I put my hands behind my head to watch. My back and shoulders burned. Too much sun, not enough sunscreen. I thought about the day ahead, hanging out with two little kids instead of one. But like Nana Grace always says, maybe I was borrowing trouble. Mica's dad would probably make her go to fun camp with him. I know mine would make me go.

I listened to the ropes creak as the houseboat tugged at its moorings. It must be blowing pretty good, I thought.

I rolled up on my side. In his bunk across the room my brother breathed through his mouth. He sounded like a purring cat. Underneath that sound, I heard a hum followed by a splash. "That's the bilge pump," Dad had said the night before at supper. "Anything that floats leaks a little. When the water reaches a certain level the pump kicks on." I was glad to hear it doing its job.

I climbed out of bed, being careful not to wake Cody up, and stepped into my shorts. I snagged a clean T-shirt out of the suitcase and snuck out of the cabin.

On the dinette in the galley was a platter of pancakes and a note.

Gone to work. Heat pcakes in toaster oven. See you boys later.

Mom

Munching cold pancake, I stepped out onto the porch of the houseboat. It was warm in spite of the wind, not like home where even warm winter days started with a jacket. I sat in the rocker that looked like Cass's and pulled my knees up.

I was thinking about getting my rod and casting to see what was in the canal, when I heard the hatch of the *Martina* slide. I wasn't ready for Mica. All I wanted to do was chew pancake and watch the water. But it wasn't the island collector who stuck a head out, it was her dad. Dr. Delano wore an outfit identical to the one he'd worn the day before, a safari getup. Seeing him, I hoped that Mica would follow, the two of them off for a fun day at fun camp.

He saw me and nodded. I nodded back. When he closed the hatch I wanted to yell, "Hey, aren't you forgetting something?" With the wind shoving the boats away from the dock, he had to pull on the stern line to get close enough to step across. Afraid he'd fall in, I almost jumped up to help him, but he made it okay. He unlocked his scooter and rolled it down the dock.

When he reached the parking lot he swung a leg over the scooter and tried to start it. All it did was sputter. "Adjust the mixture," I said quietly. Instead, he kept turning the key and kicking the starter, like one of these times it was going to work.

The sound of an engine in trouble brought Dad out from behind the building. He was wearing a pair of Uncle Bert's coveralls. Dad and Uncle Bert are about the same height, but Uncle Bert is a lot bigger in the gut. The wind blew the extra fabric out like a sail. "Want some help?" Dad wiped his hands on a rag as he walked over. "Sounds like your mixture needs adjusting." He shook Dr. Delano's hand, then rolled the scooter over to the shop side of the building.

In a minute I heard the high whine of a small engine. Dr. Delano shot out from behind the store. He jetted across the lot, veered hard right at the road, then sped over the bridge. After the buzz of the scooter died out, the only sound was the clink of the rigging hardware banging against the mast of the Delano's sailboat.

I spotted some fish floating like sticks just below the surface.

When I went back for a second pancake, I picked up the fish card instead of my rod. "Atlantic Needlefish," I said, making a match. They were probably bigger in The Islands.

A pelican skimmed along the canal, cruising so low its wing tips almost brushed the water. The needlefish spooked and darted for cover under the *Martina.*

Across the canal, two men in white uniforms marched out of the Coast Guard station, raised the flag, saluted it, and marched back inside.

I stretched and yawned—then about choked on my tongue. My whole view of the marina had suddenly been blotted out by a pterodactyl. I felt a breeze as it backpedaled with its wings. Clawed feet reached for my heart. At the last possible second the claws locked onto the porch rail. Gigantic wings folded with a rattle.

That's when I realized that it wasn't a pterodactyl. "Slip-In-Easy?" I squeaked.

The bird pegged me with one beady eye.

"Slip, is that you?" It swung its killer-sharp beak and stared at me with the other eye. The bird was big like Dad had said, and white like he'd said. It had yellow legs.

What Dad had forgotten to mention was how mean Slip looked. I hoped it was just for show. Rocky DeGarza, one of Dad's backyard guys, had put me wise to that when some older kids at school were pushing me around. "Listen, kid," he said, poking me in the chest. "You want respect, you gotta have the look, like can't nobody mess wit' choo." He pumped his fingers against my chest, to be sure he had my attention, then gripped the back of my neck and squeezed. "Listen," he breathed into my face. "You gotta have the big *A.* You gotta have the Attitude."

For a while I walked around like I had a serious case of the big *A.* Mom told me to stand up straight and get my hair out of my eyes. But this bird was the real deal. It even had a white line on its beak, like a scar. This bird was *all* Attitude.

"Hey. Don't you be givin' me the big *A*," I said, doing my best Rocky DeGarza imitation. "Wipe that sneer off your beak. I'm the nephew of the folks who feed you, so that makes me family. Now, what do you say, Slip? Want some pancake?"

The bird switched eyes again.

I tore a corner off the pancake. "Come on, take it." But the only thing that moved were a couple of feathers fluttering in the breeze.

"What? You don't like it because it's whole wheat?" I rocked forward in the chair so he could take a better look. "Aunt Emma probably feeds you the rubbery white kind, but really, this is not half bad." I reached out, wondering how heron feeding worked. Would Slip open up so I could drop the pancake in? Would he take it out of my hand or spear it with his sharp beak? In case he tried the spearing thing, I let the pancake dangle.

I was just inches from the beak when Slip's wings snapped out and the beak opened. *Skrrraaaaaaak.* The hair on my arms stood up.

Skrrraaaaaaak. With a twist of his long neck Slip dove off the rail and swooped down the canal. He landed on the dock in front of the gas pumps.

When I turned around Cody was in the open houseboat door rubbing his eyes. "Wuz that Slip?" He was still in his PJs, barefoot, his hair spiked up in back. "I want to feed him."

"Get your clothes on and we'll go give it a try."

He walked to the rail and stared at the *Martina.* "Is that girl up yet?"

"Nah, bossing us around must've worn her out."

"Wasn't that amazing the way she dove right off the mast? Even Jemmie wouldn't have the guts to do that, I bet. And now I can do underwater somersaults since she showed me how. Maybe she'll teach me how to jump off the mast, do you think? Can we go knock on her boat and get her up?"

"No, we can't knock on her boat."

"Please?"

"I said, no, and I meant it." My brother had *definitely* found himself a new hero.

We walked toward the marina store. Dad was banging on something on the far side of the building. Cody carried a pancake. "Where's Slip?" he asked, when we reached the gas pumps.

"Gee, I don't know," I said. "It only took you an hour to put your shorts on the right way around, and eat a pancake, and mash your hair down in back."

"But I *really* wanted to feed him." He looked pretty pitiful standing there holding his pancake.

"Bet you could feed those guys." I pointed out a couple of gulls sitting on the pilings. "Tear a piece off and toss it."

Best-case scenario, it would drop in the water and a bird would pick it up. But the chunk of pancake was still on its way up when the gull swooped off the piling and caught it in midair. "This is so cool!" Cody yelled. He tore the pancake in half a dozen pieces and threw them one at a time. Not one hit the water. "How'd you know they'd do that?" he asked as we walked the rest of the way to the store. I gave him a knowing shrug.

We stopped on the back deck of the store to look at the shrimp. We leaned our arms on the cool cement lip of the tank. The shrimp were mostly hanging on the sides, lots of them clustered around the bubbler. Inside, Mom was talking to someone.

"You caught on so quickly!" she said. "I gave up on trying to teach Ben and Cody."

Cody tried to touch a shrimp. "Who's Mom talking to?" he asked as the shrimp dove for the bottom.

"How about if we go see?" I held the door for him.

Mom's Tibetan bell earrings jangled as she turned her head. "Good morning, boys."

Mica was perched on a stool on the opposite side of the sales counter. Her hair looked slept in, funny in back, like Cody's. A baggy

T-shirt hung off one shoulder showing the strap of yesterday's blue swimsuit. Maybe she wore it to bed.

Mom grabbed Cody's arm as he walked by. She kissed the side of his neck, then lifted his shirt. "More sunscreen for you guys today."

"Mom!" Cody squirmed. "You're showing her my parts!"

Mica ignored his parts.

"You brothers sure do sleep late." She reached for one of the sheets of origami paper scattered on the counter.

"We've been up a long time," I said.

Mica made a snoring sound and folded the paper. "I'm helping your mother make Christmas cranes." The cranes were Mom's latest Christmas tree theme idea. When Mica had made the last fold she held up the finished crane. "How's this one, Mrs. Floyd?"

"Perfect," said Mom.

If you asked me, it looked no better or worse than the dozen others already lying on the counter, but Mom pushed the pack of paper toward Mica. "I think you're ready for a metallic."

"Jeez, a metallic." Cody sounded stunned. "You hear that, Ben?"

Mom's package of origami paper had lots of sheets of turquoise, pink, yellow, and green, but only a few of foil paper. The only thing rarer was the prints. With our injured-looking cranes, me and Cody had never gotten anywhere near the metallics.

Mica put a finger on a sheet. "Gold?" she asked, looking up at Mom.

I butted in. "Take silver or copper or gold. Take whatever one you want." But Mica seemed to need Mom's approval.

"Of course you may have gold." Mom leaned across the counter and smoothed a hand over Mica's scruffy hair. "You're doing such a wonderful job."

Mica beamed like a sheet of gold origami paper. She picked up a sheet and rubbed it against her cheek.

"Here." Mom held out a hole-punch. "You boys can do the holes and add the strings."

"What are we going to hang them *on?*" I asked. "Christmas is only a couple of days away."

"I don't know yet." My mother eyed the display rack where the hats hung. I could almost see the gears turning—the rack was sort of tree-shaped.

"Mom...," I warned. "Don't even think about it."

"You got your tree up?" Cody asked Mica.

"No." Mica bent a wing down and pressed it with her palm. "We don't do trees."

"Don't do trees?" Cody looked confused. "Why not?"

"We don't do Christmas."

"Don't do— But Santa still comes, right?"

Mom and I looked at each other. Here comes the truth about the fat man, I thought.

But Mica just flicked her bangs out of her eyes and folded the other wing. "I don't think I'm on his list anymore. We move around so much he can't keep track of me."

"B...but, Santa knows everything!" my brother sputtered. Cody wasn't where he was supposed to be either.

"Don't worry," I told him. "Mom sent a change of address form to the North Pole before we left Tallahassee."

Mom nodded. "That's exactly what I did."

"You shoulda done that too, Mica." He leaned across the counter and whispered loudly, "Mom, can Mica share our Christmas?"

"She already is," said Mom. "She's helping make the decorations."

"I mean all of it."

"First we need a tree," I repeated.

"Details, schmeetails," Mom said.

Cody let out a sigh. "I wish we'd get a real one, just this one time."

We go through this every year. Mom hates artificial trees because they're so fake, and she hates real ones because living things shouldn't have to die so people can celebrate Christmas. Her solutions to the problem are pretty lame. She bought pines in pots until we ran out of places in the yard to plant them. Last year we decorated a houseplant.

For a real Christmas tree I have to go to Cass's. Even though the rest of the year the Bodines spend as little as possible, they have the biggest light display and the best Christmas tree in the neighborhood. Picking the tree is a big deal. Mr. Bodine loads the family in the truck and rattles out to a tree farm so they can cut their own. I usually manage to be at their house on Christmas tree day. "What's your Mom decorating this year, Ben?" Mr. Bodine asks every Christmas.

Last year I had to admit, "She's got a rosemary plant in a pot, sir."

Mr. Bodine forgot that he didn't like to smile. In fact he went right past smile and laughed out loud before he remembered and turned it into a cough. "Well, son, I guess you better hop in back with the girls and help us pick out ours."

We walked over acres of planted pines before Mrs. Bodine found the perfect tree. I cut the tree down myself, then helped decorate it. I got so carried away I gave Cass her present that afternoon. She put her house key on the sneaker key chain right away.

This year I missed Christmas tree day because I had basketball practice. Now, as I punched a hole in a paper crane, I wondered what her dad would think when he saw the necklace. What if he got the wrong idea and decided I was the kind of guy he'd rather leave home on Christmas tree day? Maybe I should call Cass and tell her I mixed up her present with the one for my mom.

"Stupid string!" Cody threw a crane and the ball of string on the floor. He knew how to make a bow, but he couldn't figure out how to do the loop for the ornaments, so he stamped around the postcard rack. "Can't we do something *fun* for a change?"

"This *is* fun," said Mica. "*Way* fun." Mom had just given her the ultimate—a sheet of green-and-yellow print paper.

"No, it's not." Cody stomped on the string with his bare foot.

"Quiet," said Mica. Without even looking, she kicked him in the butt. "You'll make me mess up."

"Ben? Did you see what she did, Ben?"

Suddenly I was his protector again. "See what?" I asked.

"Don't be a baby, Cody." Mica held out the printed-paper crane. "You can be the first to look at my crane." Cody, who liked being first at anything, reached for it, but she snatched it back. "Look, don't touch. Isn't it beautiful?"

Cody rubbed his butt. "Yeah…I guess."

Mica set the crane on the counter as if it was made of glass. "Mrs. Floyd?"

Mom looked up from her own crane and took a deep breath. She put a hand on her chest, like she was about to faint. "Exquisite!" she said. "Perfect!"

Mom was already way overdoing it, but Mica waited a moment more, just to be sure there were no more compliments coming. Then she asked, "Can I hang it on your tree when you get one?"

"*If* we get one," I mumbled. I didn't like her worming her way into our Christmas.

Cody whined, "Are we *ever* gonna do *anything* on this vacation?"

Mom said, "Chill, Cody. You can't expect to be entertained all the time."

"*All* the time?" he moaned. "How about *some* of the time?"

"I have an idea, Mrs. Floyd." Mica turned to my brother and put her hands on her knees. She bent toward him and lowered her voice. "You want to do something fun, Cody? I mean like extra-extra fun?"

"Extra-extra fun?" My brother's face cracked into a wide grin. "Now you're talkin'."

"Good, because if it's okay with your mom, I'm going to take you out in my Zodiac and show you the secret tunnel I found last year. You'll be one of the few people in the whole entire world who knows about it."

"What's a Zodiac?"

"You'll see."

He looked over his shoulder at me and lowered his voice too. "What about Ben? Is he coming?" I could tell that he wanted me along—and then, at the same time, he didn't. If he went alone he'd know some colossal secret I didn't.

I gave them that couldn't-care-less face that works every time.

"Let's let him come," Cody said.

"Okay." Mica hopped off the stool. "You coming, Ben?"

For a second I acted like I was thinking it over. But sure, I was going. Secret tunnel? I'd been covering the same ground for years. I knew for a fact there wasn't a secret anything back home. No matter what the other kids did over Christmas—even if Leroy grew an inch—I'd have something to top it.

"Not so fast, guys," Mom said. "Clear it with Dad first."

"What are we waiting for?" Cody dashed for the door. "Let's ask him!"

"Cody?" Mica tapped her foot and pointed down.

"What?" He pretended like he didn't see the string and crane on the floor.

"Your mother doesn't want to pick up after you."

Cody scuffed a bare foot on the concrete floor. "Oh, she doesn't mind."

"Oh, yes she does." Mom hung an arm over Mica's shoulders. It was like Mom had a daughter all of a sudden. They even looked a little alike.

"I'll ask Dad," I said. I let the screen door slam as I went out to the shop.

chapter ten

THE SECRET TUNNEL

"It looks like a wading pool," whispered Cody, staring down at
the gray rubber craft that bumped the piling. The Zodiac had
inflated sides, but it was no wading pool. It looked like something commandos would use for a night landing on an enemy beach.

Mica sprang from the dock to the Zodiac and held up her arms.
"I'll take the provisions, Mrs. Floyd." Mom handed down the cooler.

"What did you pack us for drinks?" Cody asked.

"Water and juice," Mom said.

He gave her his best puppy face. "No sodas?"

"It's against her religion," I said, passing Mica the bag of apples.

"How about chips, Mom? Pleasey please," Cody begged. "We're
on vacation."

"Aunt Emma gave me chips all the time," Mica said.

"See, Mom. Aunt Emma thinks chips are okay."

But Mom just put her arms around Cody and hugged him against
her. "Mom to Cody's body: are you ready for a big blast of salt and
grease?" Then she made her voice high, like Cody's body was answer-
ing back. "No thank you, ma'am. I'd prefer an apple."

Cody made his voice high too. "This is the *real* Cody's body
speaking. I'm starving for salt and grease. Dying."

Mom ruffed his hair up. "Nice try, mister."

Dad came down the steps. "I hear you guys are going somewhere."

"A secret tunnel," Cody said.

I had already gotten his permission, but Dad is one of those parents who has to check everything out. He dropped to his heels on the dock. "How's your safety gear, captain?"

"It's great, sir." Mica opened a metal box on the floor. "We have Band-Aids, salve, a tourniquet, a snakebite kit. Here's the flashlight." She mashed the On button, then shook the flashlight until it lit. "Works fine, see? And here's an emergency flare for if we get lost after dark."

Cody stopped yearning for chips. "We're gonna get lost in the dark?"

Mica reached up and patted his bare foot. "Of course not. But you have to be prepared. Right, Mr. Floyd?"

"I don't see your PFDs," my father said.

Cody blushed. "Jeez, Dad... You're not supposed to see our underwear."

I gave him a shove. "That's BVDs, doofus."

"A PFD is a personal flotation device," Mica explained. "I swim like a fish. I don't need one."

"These landlubbers do," Dad said, giving me a shove like the one I'd given Cody, only harder. "Besides, you won't make it past the Coast Guard station without 'em. You know that, Mica." He went over to a box on the dock and opened the lid.

I was thinking that a personal flotation device sounded like something James Bond might wear. Pull a cord, it self-inflates. The sun goes down, it glows in the dark. But Dad came back with three orange life jackets just like the ones we wore when we went out with Dewey—only bad smelling. When he dropped mine over my head the back of my neck felt creepy and damp, like I was wearing a wet cat.

I thought Mica would refuse to wear a wet cat, but she did all the ties and buckles without a peep. She even thanked Dad. She was really kissing up.

Before we could climb aboard, Dad made Mica tell him exactly where she was taking us. "Down the creek," she said. "Past Venetian Shores, but before you reach the bay. Not far at all."

"No added trips oceanside," Dad warned. "It's rough as a cob, and I wouldn't let you take a Zodiac out there even if it was dead calm."

"We'd be okay," Mica assured him. "Zodiacs are rescue craft. They're perfectly safe in rough seas…" But she must have seen that with Dad, getting away from the dock was the rough part. "Okay," she said. "We'll stay in the creek." She squatted in the stern and started the motor. "Come on, brothers. Let's hit it!" I climbed down, then gave Cody a hand. We parked ourselves on the wooden seat that straddled the pontoons.

Dad untied the line but held onto it. "Mica, I'm trusting you to bring these two guys back in good shape." Then he dropped the line in the bow and tapped his watch. "No later than noon, understand?"

She gave him a dumb salute. "Understood, sir."

"Noon?" I sputtered. "You're kidding, right?" He tapped the watch again. "What about you and cousin Bob fishing all night?"

"That was different." He gave our bow a push, then grinned. "We didn't have me for a dad. And Cody," he added as I turned away from him in disgust. "You listen to Mica. She's in charge."

I whipped back around. "Thought *I* was in charge of Cody."

"Not today, bud."

"Why not? I do a good job of looking out for him. He's still alive, isn't he?"

"This is Mica's territory," he called above the whine of the motor. "If you're smart, you'll listen to her too."

Listen to her, my foot.

Mom called, "Bon voyage!" Mica and Cody waved like crazy.

My hands stayed in my lap. So far nothing at Bert's Marina was living up to Dad's stories.

We idled at the mouth of the canal. Across the creek at Pirate's Bay Resort, a man sat at the dockside bar, playing guitar, one foot on a sleeping dog. To our left loomed the massive concrete bridge pilings. To our right, Snake Creek wound toward the bay.

Mica watched a strand of seaweed drift past. "Tide's going out."
She eased the Zodiac into the creek. Under the bridge the Atlantic
was dotted with whitecaps. Birds sat on the channel markers, feathers ruffed up. Foam piled the sandbars on either side of the channel.

"Rough as a cop," Cody said.

"Cob," I corrected.

"That's what I said. Rough as a cop."

As kids, Dad and cousin Bob would've motored under the bridge
and headed for the horizon. Not us. We had to answer to the grown-
up Dad.

Using the handle attached to the motor to steer, Mica turned the
Zodiac away from the bridge.

But even in the sheltered creek, water slapped rubber. Spray spit
in our faces. For the first time since putting it on, I could smell something besides the stink of my PFD: salt and seaweed. I tried to
remember what the air smelled like at home, but I guess I was too
used to it to remember. I caught myself leaning forward, like there
was something great up ahead.

Bigger boats passed. Each threw a wake that rocked us. Compared
to the thrum of the big boat's engines, the Zodiac's motor sounded
like a mosquito. We were rolling over the wake of a huge sport fisherman called *Ace High* when Cody announced, "My stomach feels
funny."

"No, it doesn't," Mica told him.

"Trust me, it does," I said. "If you barf, Cody, remember who's in
charge." I was feeling better by the minute.

On the right bank of the wide creek were fancy houses built on
canals. They had decks and picnic tables with umbrellas. Powerboats
hung from metal arms Mica called davits. The only trees were tall
palms. The yards were white gravel. It looked like something off TV.
"Civilization," Mica sniffed, and steered for the opposite shore.

We putted along just a few feet from the thicket of trees that grew
right out of the water. "Red mangroves," she said. "Latin name,
Rhizophora mangle."

"They look like a bunch of giant spiders," Cody said.

Mica turned off the motor and grabbed one of the leggy roots so we could get a better look. Even peering far back into the thicket, we couldn't see dry land, just the mangrove's spider-leg roots, all knotted and woven together with shallow water running between them.

"Mangroves are the island builders," Mica lectured. "They catch dead leaves and seaweed and sand and turn them into solid land." Only half listening, I counted three lures hanging on distant branches. Next time out, I'd bring a rod. Even with a miniature, know-it-all tour guide, I was still in the Keys.

Mica broke off a leaf and held it out to my brother. "Lick this."

Cody squeezed his eyes and mouth shut, then opened one eye. "What're those shiny things?" Sparkly crystals were glued to the back of the leaf.

She shoved the mangrove leaf in his face. "You tell me."

He turned. "Ben?"

I held up my hands. "Hey, you heard Dad. She's in charge."

And out came the tongue—Cody is always more curious than scared. "Salt," he said, after one quick lick. "Like out of a salt shaker."

"That's right, Cody. Good for you."

"Big deal," I said. "The air is salty so the leaves are salty; it's a salty place."

"Wrong!" Mica said. "For your information, mangroves secrete the salt through their leaves, like sweat."

"Great," I said. "A sweaty plant." Sitting in the crown of a mangrove a little way down the creek were three big white birds. "Great white herons," I said, to show that I knew something about the local nature too.

"Wrong again!" She was so happy I was wrong she laughed. "Hah! Those are common egrets. Check out the legs, landlubber. They're black. Great white heron's legs are yellow."

"You can't even see their legs."

Mica stood up in the stern. "Hey, egrets," she yelled. "Show Ben your legs!"

The crown of the mangrove wobbled. One by one, the birds spread their wings and flew.

Black legs.

Black legs.

Black. Darn. Couldn't there have been even one pair of yellow legs in the bunch?

The egrets turned to small specks against the sky. Mica restarted the motor. As we pulled away from the mangroves, Cody lunged for the side of the Zodiac. "Hey, look at that!" A shiny pink and blue balloon-thing was drifting toward us. "Somebody help me catch it!"

"Are you nuts?" Mica slapped the back of his head. "That's a Portuguese man-of-war. Under that balloon is a mess of tentacles that sting like fire."

"Oh." Cody rubbed the spot on the back of his head. "You could've just said."

Maybe Dad had a point. If Mica hadn't been with us, I would've been helping Cody grab the balloon.

We motored along in silence a while, then Mica shaded her eyes. "There it is!"

"There what is?" All I saw was more water, more sky, and more mangroves.

Cody strained forward, mouth open. "I don't see nothing."

"Are you blind?" She slapped the back of his head again.

"Quit slapping him," I said.

"I want him to open his eyes. There, Cody. See? That's it!"

Cody looked confused. "*What's* it?"

"The entrance to the tunnel. Right there."

He still didn't see it. I didn't see it either.

"It'll be a tight fit," she said, "but we can make it." We were real close before I realized that what looked like a shady spot was actually a narrow opening between the mangroves. Mica slipped our boat in like a thread through the eye of a needle and shut off the motor.

As we pulled into the tunnel, the air got still. "This is a hurricane creek." Mica's voice was hushed. She stood and used an overhead branch to pull the boat along. "In the olden days people brought their boats into the creeks to ride out storms."

"They must've had awful small boats," I said.

She reached for the next branch. "This is just a little creek. Some are big enough to shelter a boat the size of the *Martina*."

"Yeah? And I guess they're longer too." Just ahead was an impenetrable mangrove wall. Mica's big-deal secret tunnel was about thirty feet long. I'd make it longer when I told the guys.

"This one's plenty long," she said, continuing to drag the boat toward the dead end.

"World class," I said. Once I wrote a report about the Middle Ages. I drew a torture device called an iron maiden on the cover. The iron maiden was a box with knives in the lid. They'd stuff the prisoner in the box. The torture part happened when the lid closed.

Mica kept heading for the wall of mangrove branches, all of which seemed to be aimed at Cody and me. "Mica... We might want to turn back about now."

"Why?" We were within a heartbeat of being skewered when Mica swung the boat to the right and forced it into an even skinnier passage.

Branches squealed against rubber. "Ben?" Cody breathed in my ear. "The Zodiac is kind of like a big balloon, isn't it?"

"I guess."

"What if it...pops?"

A branch broke against the hull with a loud snap. Cody jumped.

"You know, you guys *could* help me," Mica said.

I stood up and grabbed a branch.

Cody tugged the leg of my trunks. "Ben, what if we get stuck?"

"Ask captain kid."

"Quit being a wimp, Cody," the kid in charge said.

"I'm not a wimp, okay? I'm just saying, what if?" Cody's voice quivered. "You know how a cork gets jammed in a bottle? Like that. I mean, what if?"

Mica pulled so hard the branches screeched against the sides—

chalk on blackboard times ten. "If you want to be safe, sit on the sofa for the rest of your life."

Cody was quiet for a few seconds. "Could I have a TV?" he asked in a small voice.

"Sure," she answered. "That way you can watch other people's adventures. You won't have any of your own."

We had been at it for at least an hour. Twigs and sticks littered the Zodiac. Mica had leaves in her hair. My T-shirt was soaked with sweat. But if she was waiting for me to say I give up, it wasn't going to happen. Let *her* admit she was licked, then we'd back out.

In the meantime, I was sort of enjoying the torture. About now the big excitement back home would be baking cookies with Nana Grace, fighting over who got to eat the busted ones.

"Break time," Mica said suddenly. She flopped down in the bottom and rested her head against the inflated side of the Zodiac. Her eyes closed.

I'd seen this move before. Mica was beat, but she couldn't admit it. She'd let some time pass. When we started again—surprise!—we'd be going the other way.

Cody passed out apples and bottles of water. "Sure wish we had some chips," he said, setting an apple on Mica's stomach.

"What did you mean when you said Aunt Emma gave you chips?" I asked.

"Chips, candy bars, gum—she gave me pretty much anything I wanted."

I hated to ask, afraid to find out. "Is she really your aunt?"

"Well, no. But she's just like one. I hung out with her a lot last year. I helped her in the store on weekends when the Captain and I weren't at fun camp."

Like an aunt. I relaxed. Out on the creek, the pitch of an engine rose as a boat picked up speed. Cars rumbled across the bridge in the distance. Except for the occasional crunch of an apple, it was silent inside the tunnel.

Cody rested his head next to Mica's and shut his eyes too. They acted like they were asleep, but every now and then one of them lifted an apple and took a bite.

I was about to stretch out myself when I heard a scratching noise. I turned my head quick, but there was nothing there.

Mica rolled onto her stomach. "Keep your eyes open," she whispered.

"Thanks for the advice," I whispered back.

She put her finger to her lips and sat up slowly. I was just thinking that it was probably a couple of branches scraping together when I heard it again.

"There," Mica whispered, as a speckled crab appeared out of the shadows. "It's a mangrove crab." The crab walked sideways along a branch. *"Aratus pisonii.* They spend their whole lives in the mangroves. To a mangrove crab the whole universe is just an endless maze of roots."

"Boring neighborhood," I whispered back. The red-and-white specked crab tapped along, moving slowly through shifting patches of light. I liked the way the sun made the stiff, waxy leaves sparkle. The water was as clear as ginger ale. Tiny fish hung like ornaments among the mangrove roots. When it comes to secret tunnels, I thought, this one isn't half-bad. I'd never seen anyplace like it. I wished Justin was here. He needed to see a few things for real, not just on the nature channel.

Cody slapped his neck. "There's mosquitoes buzzing my ears."

The mangrove crab vanished with a chattering click of its feet.

"Time to go," Mica said. I could tell by the way she said it that she wasn't talking about turning back.

As we pressed forward, deeper into the heart of the mangrove jungle, more mosquitoes found us. "They're gonna suck us dry," Cody complained. But me and Mica kept dragging the Zodiac forward. It was like a dare. Who could keep going the longest?

"When Mom and Dad find us we'll be shriveled bags of skin." My brother sounded like he was going to cry, imagining our parents finding us all flat and desiccated. "Ben, can we go back?"

"Ask the captain."

"Mica?"

Mica didn't answer.

His bottom lip quivered, then he brightened up. "Say! You think Mom'll let us have chips when she sees how bit up we are?"

We got plenty more bites, which might have been good from the chip angle, but we were all starting to itch, big-time. The raft squeaked over the knees of roots. And Cody kept asking, "Are we almost there?" as if we were on a car trip with Dad.

"Not too much farther," Mica said. Dad used that line too.

I didn't believe we were going toward anything but more bites and skinnier passages, but even though I was sure each inch we gained would be the last, I wanted to see how far we could go. Somehow, we kept taking that last inch again and again.

Then suddenly, the struggle was over. We slid out of the clutches of the mangroves. "Wow!" Cody whispered as the Zodiac spun slowly. "This is awesome!"

"Told ya," Mica whispered back as we drifted to the center of a clear, deep pool. Every leaf was mirrored on the water. The reflections wavered as we rippled the surface. "What do you say, Ben?"

"Nice. Real nice." We all talked softly. It didn't seem right to shout. The arching mangrove branches formed a high ceiling over our heads. It felt like church.

"Have you been here before?" Cody asked.

"No," Mica admitted. "I didn't get this far the last time."

"Then maybe we're the first ones to come here, ever."

Mica trailed a hand in the water. "I bet we are."

Considering how we had had to fight our way in, I was ready to agree. We had to be the first. Then I saw it. "Hey, you guys. Look!" Mica and Cody leaned over the side. Mica gasped.

"Somebody else got here." Cody swallowed hard. "But they never left!"

chapter eleven

A ONE-WAY TRIP TO THE BOTTOM

I t's been down there a long time," Mica said.
A long, long time," Cody echoed.
We leaned on our arms and watched fish dart over and under seats where passengers had once sat. Everything aboard the sunken boat was covered with a layer of silt. "That's a hammer," I said, pointing out a ghostly shape on the boat floor.

"What's that?" Cody dug his fingernails into my arm. "A hand?"

I knuckle-rubbed his head. "Quit working that imagination overtime. It's just an old glove." Nobody said it, but we were all looking for skeletons down there.

"What's that thing in the middle of the boat?" Cody asked. "The motor?"

"The boat's a dory," said Mica. "If it had a motor it'd be an outboard on the back." She brought her face so close to the water the ends of her hair got wet. "It's some kind of box. See, it's got a handle." She sat back up, hair dripping. "Treasure!" she whispered.

"Treasure?" Cody squeaked. Both of them flopped down, faces just inches from the water.

I nudged him. "Come on, bro, you know what that is." Hanging out with Dad all his life, Cody had to recognize the shape, the size, the crescent that would flip up to become a handle. But Cody was blinded by the possibility of treasure. "Sorry to give you this news flash, guys," I said. "But that's a toolbox."

"A toolbox?" Cody sounded like he'd never heard of one before.

"You sure?" Mica asked.

"I may not know an egret from a heron, but I *do* know toolboxes. And that's a toolbox."

"Oh." She put her head down, chin against the side and gazed at the toolbox. All of a sudden she sat up straight. "Of course it could have anything in it."

"Yeah," I said, "like tools."

"Or anything," she insisted. "Whatever's in it is ours. All we have to do is bring it up. It's the law of salvage."

Cody looked dreamy. "The law of salvage."

The law of salvage... Mica had to be making this stuff up.

"The law of 'finders keepers, losers weepers,'" Cody elaborated.

"What're we waiting for, brothers?" Mica yelled, "Let's go get it!"

"All right!" Cody slapped the side of the Zodiac sending a twangy echo through the rubber. He stuck a foot in the water.

I grabbed him by the life vest and pulled him back. "You can't swim."

"Can too!" he said. And we were off, yelling "Can not, can too, can not, can too."

While we argued, Mica tied the bowline around her bottle of water and lowered it until it landed on the toolbox lid. A puff of silt rose like smoke. Hand over hand, she brought the rope up again, measuring the dripping line with her arms. "Nine feet," she said. "Easy cheesy." She shed her PFD and T-shirt. Down to her swimsuit, she said, "Come on, brothers."

I undid the buckles on my own PFD. "Okay," I said. "But it's just an old toolbox."

"Treasure box," Mica corrected.

I dropped the life vest on the Zodiac floor. "All it has in it are three socket wrenches, two Allen wrenches, and a carburetor from a seventy-two Plymouth."

Mica jumped in. She held onto the oar that was locked to the side of the Zodiac and hung there. "It could be money, you know."

"Could it really be money?" Cody asked.

"Sure," said Mica. "Or gold."

"It isn't," I said, pulling my T-shirt over my head.

Cody tugged at the straps on his own PFD. "Help me off with this, Ben."

"No, bro, you stay here."

"But I wanna come! Mica!"

"You be lookout," Mica said.

Lookout? Who was going to show up? The last guys to get here were probably still on the bottom. "We need you to keep an eye on Mica and me, bro. It's not safe having all of us in the water at the same time."

"Oh, okay," he said. "I'll be the lifeguard." I slid over the side, and into the cool water without him.

Mica dove. Her straggly hair floated around her in a big billow. Each time she kicked, it streamed straight back. She lifted the tool-box handle with one finger, then used it to pull herself down. When her feet touched, her legs were swallowed in a cloud of silt. She leaned back, straining against the handle.

I took one deep breath and dove. Below, a pale green Mica was still leaning back against the handle. I kicked my way to the bottom, but my fingers had barely grazed the lid before my lungs sent my brain an urgent message. Breathe or die. I shot back up. Mica did too.

"You didn't get it," Cody said, as the two of us gasped for air.

"No shit, Sherlock," I wheezed.

"But you're gonna get it, aren't you?"

"Sure," said Mica. "Here's the plan, Ben. I'll take the far end, you take the near one."

"And what do I do?" Cody asked.

"You be ready to lift it over the side," I said.

Mica counted to three. We dove. When we reached bottom we planted our feet in the soft, slimy silt. Each of us squeezed our fingers under an end of the box. The water clouded as we tried to lift, but it was like the box was glued to the bottom.

Then, all at once, something let go and the box shot up. Mica smiled, leaking bubbles out of the corners of her mouth. But we only swam a couple feet before we dropped the box and headed for the surface. The air hit my face. I sucked in a deep breath.

"Why'd you drop it?" Mica demanded.

"Why did *I* drop it? *You* were the one who dropped it." I didn't know who had let go first—but it wasn't necessarily me.

We fanned our arms and looked down at the toolbox, which now lay on its side, handle sticking out. "Try again," Mica said.

This time we moved the box about two feet the other direction before dropping it.

"Again," she said.

The next time it landed on its other side—but in pretty much the same spot. "This isn't working," I said as we hung off the oar, catching our breath.

Cody had finally managed to take his PFD off. "I'm gonna help," he said, and he swung a leg over the side.

"No!" we both yelled.

Mica stared at me through drippy bangs. "Come on, Ben. We have to get it!" Then *bam,* her arms were around my ribs and she was trying to drag me under.

"Would you hold on a minute!" With a quick twist of my body I broke her grip. "We can keep diving on it 'til we rupture, but we'll never bring it up this way."

But the girl was stubborn. "One, two, three..."

I grabbed her by the swimsuit strap. "If it makes you happy, we'll keep going. But Christmas isn't the best time for a double-drowning." I gave her a chance to imagine lying dead on the bottom, silt settling on her eyeballs. Then I said something Dad always says when we're having trouble fixing an engine. "When all else fails, think."

"Think? I'd rather *do* something," declared Mica.

"Fine. *Do* something."

Mica impersonated a chicken. Her idea of doing something. I ignored her and looked around, wishing I had a pulley. Of course I didn't find one. "Would you cool it!" I said, and I dunked her—it's hard to think with someone clucking. Maybe I could use something else… "How long's the bowline?" I asked when she resurfaced.

"I don't know." Miss Super-Chicken looked sullen. "Twenty feet, maybe."

"Good. That'll work." I hauled myself back over the side of the Zodiac.

I scanned the mangrove branches that formed the ceiling above the pool until I found one that was thick and high. With the line still tied to the eye at the bow, I tossed the coil of rope. It hit the branch and fell in the water. I dragged it back and tried again. This time it flopped over the branch and hung low enough for me to reach it. "Here." I passed the free end to Mica. "You think you can tie that to the handle of the box?"

"If it makes you happy." She did a back roll with the rope in one hand, tied it to the handle, and came back up. I gave the rope a tug.

"What? You don't think it'll hold?" She pushed her wet hair back. "For your information, I'm a knot expert."

"World champion," I said under my breath. "Get back in the Zodiac," I told her. "We're gonna haul this thing up."

"Even me?" Cody asked.

I snapped the waist on his trunks. "Especially you. You're the only one who isn't all worn out."

We had to squish together so we could all get our hands on the rope. Cody about put out my eye with his elbow, but as we pulled, we felt the box skip across the bottom.

I ended up bracing against a couple of branches to keep the Zodiac from flipping and let the other two tow it in. Using the mechanical advantage of my sort-of pulley, the box didn't feel anywhere near as heavy.

"We're doing it, we're doing it, we're doing it," Cody sang as they lifted the treasure toolbox from the bottom. When it surfaced, I grabbed the handle and hauled it over the side.

"Open it," Cody urged. "Open it!"

"Can't," I said. "It's locked." Each of us tried pulling the lock off.

"Stand back, both of you!" Mica swung hard and smacked it with an oar. The lock was corroded, but it still worked fine. After that we sat, watching rusty water leak out the corners.

Mica lifted one side. "Too heavy for tools. Maybe it *is* gold."

"I move Dad's toolboxes all the time," I said. "They're plenty heavy." But I looked around the mangrove pool, a place that had probably only been seen by human eyes twice. "You know," I admitted. "This *would* be a good place to hide a treasure."

"Quick!" Cody said. "Let's get out of here before the guys who hid our treasure come back." He made it sound as if one-eyed pirates were hacking their way through the mangroves to get to us. Suddenly, all three of us were desperate to go.

But while we had been busy scraping through the tunnel, diving and swallowing water, the tide had kept on going out. What had been a tight squeeze on the way in was almost impossible coming out. We hung up at least a hundred times and had to stand on the mangrove roots to walk the Zodiac forward. At first Cody climbed out too, but he kept falling in. "Stay put, Cody," I said when I heard the next squeal of rubber. "You supervise." Cody knew that "supervise" meant "do nothing." He usually objected, but he was tired out. He supervised by falling asleep in the bottom of the boat.

When we finally pulled out of the tunnel the wind hit us, fresh and salty.

Cody sat up and stretched. "That was quick," he said.

Mica and I gave each other a look.

"What?" said Cody. "I wasn't sleeping."

Mica started the motor. We were halfway home before I noticed our PFDs heaped on the floor of the Zodiac. "Better put these on," I said. We'd blown Dad's noon curfew, I could tell by the position of the sun. "We're probably in enough trouble already."

We had just passed the Coast Guard station when Cody waved both arms and shouted, "Look! It's Mom and Dad!" They were waiting at the end of the dock.

Not a good sign.

"You're back!" Mom cried. She ran along beside us as we motored up the canal. "We were so worried."

"Look what we found!" Mica shouted back.

"Treasure," Cody yelled. "Gold! Right here in this box."

"Gold, huh?" Dad eyed the drippy toolbox as we pulled in behind the *Martina*. "Funny thing," he said, hoisting the box up to the dock. "Gold feels about as heavy as tools."

chapter twelve

TOOLS OR TREASURE?

"Here!" Cody hugged a chunk of coral rock he'd found lying at the edge of the canal. "Bust it open with this, Dad."

"Are you nuts?" Mica asked, looking around. "What if it *is* gold? Do you really want to open it out here, where anyone can see?"

"This calls for secrecy," said Dad, playing along. He carried the toolbox into the store and set it on a chair. While he went for a hammer and Mom ran to the houseboat to get the camera, Cody and Mica stared at the box. "Brothers," Mica whispered, putting an arm around each of our necks. "Before your father opens this box we have to swear, *I mean swear,* that no matter what's inside, we'll split it three ways or hope to die. Okay?"

"Three ways or hope to die." Cody never took his eyes off the box.

"Shake on it," she said. And she and Cody shook hands solemnly.

"Ben?" Mica held out her hand. "Three ways or hope to die?"

I shook her hand, then Cody's. "Three ways. Sure, whatever."

"And hope to die?" she said, like not saying it gave me a loophole.

Dad raised the hammer. "Now?"

"Just a sec." Mom fiddled with the lens. "Wait, I forgot to turn on the flash."

"My arm's getting tired, Samantha Jean."

"Okay, all set."

Dad brought the hammer down. *Wham!* The flash fired. The lock flew across the room. It nicked a Styrofoam cooler, then clattered to a stop against a rack of sunglasses. Dad rubbed his hands. "Let's see what we've got." While Cody and Mica shoved each other trying to get the first look, Dad gave me a wink.

I stayed back, acting cool. I could see over their shoulders.

"This is it," said Dad as he lifted the hasp. But the hinges were rusty and the lid stayed shut. The suspense was driving me crazy. Dad tapped the hinges with the hammer, then sprayed them with penetrating oil. Even though I knew there was about zero percent chance of finding gold in an old toolbox, I could hear my heartbeat in my ears.

The odds are bad on the lottery too, but I know a kid at school whose cousin's friend won the jackpot. Four million dollars.

"Let's try that again," Dad said, and he cracked his knuckles.

The hinges moaned as the lid slowly opened. Cody and Mica pushed in. They got their eyes right next to the widening gap. Mom's flash fired again, lighting the inside of the box.

"Holy Toledo!" Dad shouted. "Isn't this dandy!"

I quit holding my breath.

Mica slumped as if someone had let the air out of her.

"Is that all?" said Cody, leaning against Mica.

"What do you mean, is that all?" Dad hollered. "This is great! We'll clean these tools up and they'll be good as new. I'll bet your dad would like some of them, Mica."

"You keep 'em." She wandered over and gave the hat rack a slap that set it spinning.

Dad whistled as he sorted tools. For him, Santa had already come.

As the hats spun, Mica's eyes got glassy. Watching Mica, Mom's eyes got shiny too. How could Mom not see that Mica was acting bratty and spoiled? The old quivering lip would've gotten Cody or me exactly nowhere, but it was working for Mica Delano. Mom walked over and put her arms around Mica, who buried her head in the front of Mom's blouse.

"Family hug!" Cody shouted. He threw his arms around Mica from behind. "Dad? Ben?"

The family hug is a Cody invention. It's when every available Floyd piles on until we become a single mass of family. It's embarrassing. Even when it's just us. Dad spread his arms. "Come on, Floyds! What can we do to cheer this girl up?"

"We can tell her to get over it," I mumbled. Sure, Mica was disappointed, but so was Cody, so was I. Why was it our job to cheer her up? Mica was like the tar baby. Everyone but me was getting stuck to her.

"I know," said Mom, in her best cheerful-Mom voice. "I'll make you a French braid."

Bingo. Mica turned off the waterworks. "What's a French braid?"

Mom pulled a comb out of her skirt pocket. "I'll show you."

"Wait." Mica put her hands over her tangled, salty hair. "I have to do something first." She bolted out of the store and down the back steps.

In a minute she streaked through with a towel and shampoo in her arms. We heard the water running in the shower behind the shop.

Dad pulled the last tool out of the box, then whistled through his teeth. "Take a look at this!" He reached in one last time, and held up something he'd found at the very bottom. "Give this to Mica, Ben. It'll definitely cheer her up."

I fell back a step. "Nuh-uh. Not me." What was it? Did I suddenly have "guy who gives girls jewelry" printed on my forehead?

"Me, me!" Cody snatched the chain with the tarnished silver charm on it. "I'll give it to her."

"Let me do her hair first," Mom said. "Then you can give it to her."

Cody polished the charm with his T-shirt, then put the chain over his own head. He was stuffing it inside his shirt when Mica came in from the shower.

I thought he would bust, waiting to give her the necklace, because the French braid took a while. Mom had to comb the knots out and braid hair that was all different lengths. Mica tugged at a short piece. "I tried to give myself a haircut," she explained.

Eventually, Mom conquered.

Cody poked Mom in the back. "Can I give it to her *now?*"

"Go ahead."

"This is for you." My brother reached inside his T-shirt. "It was in our box. At the bottom." She gasped when she saw the little dolphin, then grabbed the chain and wiggled it up past his ears. "Ow!" he said, then grinned. "See, there really was a treasure."

"Mrs. Floyd?" She handed the necklace to Mom, who undid the catch and put it around her neck. The dolphin hung beside the wedding ring and the shower key.

"You're barracuda bait for sure," I said.

Mom took Mica by the shoulders and steered her over to the chrome bait freezer. Mica stared at her own wavery reflection, not smiling.

"You really need to see the back of your hair," Mom fussed. "That's the good part. Guys, we need another mirror." There was a tiny mirror on the sunglass display. Dad dragged the rack over. Standing on a cinderblock to make herself taller, Mica got a sort-of look at her French braid. "Aren't you pretty?" Mom said, squeezing her shoulders.

"You really think so?" Mica said softly. She touched the dolphin charm with one finger. This time her reflection smiled. It wasn't a big smile—you couldn't see teeth or anything—but it was a smile.

Mom smoothed the sides of Mica's hair one last time. "Better?"

Mica nodded, then touched Mom's hair. "Better. Now you need one too."

"Good idea." Mom did her own hair in a French braid. "Now we look alike," Mom said, even though her braid was long and thick and smooth and Mica's had short pieces jabbing out all over the place.

"We should go somewhere and show our hair off," Mica said.

"How about the Winn Dixie," Mom suggested. "We need a few vegetables."

Mica got all excited about showing her hair off at the grocery store. "Just give me two seconds," she said, and she dashed to the *Martina* again. When she came back this time she wore shorts over her swimsuit. Dangling from each hand was a rubber flip-flop, both so worn-out they had holes in the heels. She slapped them together. "Cody, Ben, let's go."

"Think I'll pass," I said. Cody and Mica scampered after Mom out to Aunt Emma's pickup—an automatic, so Mom could drive it.

"How about giving me a hand cleaning these tools?" Dad said.

"You sure you wouldn't rather wait for Mica?"

He tossed a rag at me. "Green-eyed monster got you, Ben?"

I caught the rag and picked up a pair of pliers. "Me, jealous of Mica? Are you kidding?" I concentrated on the pliers. "She just makes me mad. That crying scene was so bogus. She really had you and Mom going though."

"Because we made a fuss over her? Come on, Ben, who does it hurt? Mica just needs a little attention."

"Give me a break, Dad. Mica's life is totally cool. She sails around the world, she doesn't go to school. Her dad doesn't crowd her. She's totally self-sufficient."

"Self-sufficient like your buddy, Justin? That just means their folks leave 'em alone too much."

"Justin's fine. He watches whatever he wants on TV. Nobody gets on him about anything. He can eat macaroni and cheese every night if he feels like it."

I expected a big lecture, but all he said was, "Bet he gets awful tired of macaroni and cheese."

"We got one!" Cody whooped, running into the marina store. "A real one!"

I looked up from the socket wrench I was wiping down. "A real what?"

"A real, truly-life Christmas tree!"

Mom and Mica followed Cody in, dragging the tree.

"Well, Samantha Jean," Dad said, putting his knuckles on his hips. "What in the world came over you?"

"They were half price," Mom said.

"And the man with the truck by the side of the road said he had to get back to Michigan in time for Christmas," Cody added. "He has two kids."

"It was already cut down…," Mom said. Like we hadn't tried that argument out on her every other year.

"And Mica wanted it," Cody said. "She was teeny tiny the last time her family had a tree. She was wishing for one."

"Does that mean you used to 'do' Christmas?" I asked.

"Sure." Mica kicked off a flip-flop and caught it. "Before my mother started touring all the time we did. Our trees were twelve feet tall with millions of lights."

"This one's only half that tall," Mom said.

"But it's beautiful." Mica put an arm around my mother's waist.

"Splendiferous!" Dad assured her.

"Better than any old houseplant. It even smells like Christmas!" Cody sniffed the needles, then yelped when they poked him in the nose.

"We'll decorate it tonight," Mom said. "Mica, see if your father will let you come help."

"Don't worry, I'll be there." She kicked the second flip-flop so high it smacked the ceiling.

chapter thirteen

DECK THE BOAT

We had veggie burgers for dinner. Mom had brought the powdered veggie stuff from home. It's lumpy and gross looking, but it tastes okay—or maybe I'm just used to it from being vegetarian all my life. Or mostly vegetarian. Every once in a while Dad takes me and Cody to McDonald's or some other fast food place. We pile our trays with Big Macs and fries and shakes and chow down. We always end up with stomachaches we can't tell Mom about.

Most of the time being vegetarian is okay, but as I took a bite of modified soy I wondered if I would be taller if I ate burgers and pot roast and all the other stuff Mom calls the American death-diet.

Cody elbowed me. "Look! There she is!" Mica was prowling around on the shallow side of the dock just outside the window. A floating bucket bumped her shins. She had a net in one hand.

"Can't we ever get away from her?" I asked.

"You *are* away from her," Dad said. "She's not out there because of us."

"Like fun she isn't."

Mica dipped something up with the net, stared at what she'd caught, then dropped it in the bucket. "Can I go see what she got?" Cody asked.

"Finish your supper first," Mom said.

Mica took a sly glance at our window.

"See what I mean, Dad? See what I mean?" I hissed.

But by the time he looked she was dipping up another something.

"Mom…? Cody begged. "I'll be quick like a bunny."

"Why don't you invite Mica in for a burger? Then you can ask her what she's putting in the bucket."

"She already ate," I said. "I saw her heating something up at the picnic table."

Cody dragged a bite of burger through the puddle of tamari on his plate. "Sea rations," he said.

"What do you mean, sea rations?" Mom asked.

"Canned stuff."

"Canned stuff?" Mom slid the window open. "Mica, honey? Do you want to join us for a little supper?"

Mica acted all surprised that we were there—even Mom, who could be fooled by anyone, had to see she was faking it. "Sure," Mica called. "Just let me put these specimens in the tank." And she held up the bucket to show she really *had* been doing something besides spying.

"What'd you get?" Cody asked as soon as she let herself in.

"An anemone and a seahorse."

"A seahorse?" Cody looked at Mom. "Please, can I go see?"

"Veggie burger first," Mom said. "And how about one for you, Mica?"

"Actually, I already ate."

Cody said, "Sea rations, right?"

"Canned stew." Mica sniffed. "It smells good in here, but not like burgers."

"It's veggie burgers," Cody said. "They're just like regular burgers without the bun or the ketchup. Oh, yeah, no meat either."

"I've never had a veggie burger," she said.

"Then you should try one." Mom got out an extra plate and some silverware.

Mica ignored the fork. She broke a piece off with her fingers and stuffed it in her mouth. Come on, Mom, I thought, give her the manners lecture. But Mom failed me.

"Well?" said Mom. "How do you like it?"

Mica shoved another chunk of soy in her mouth. "Interesting. It tastes so uncanned!"

"Un-canned?" Mom laughed. "I'll take that as a compliment." She added salad to Mica's plate. "So, Mica, can you stay to decorate the tree?"

"Oh sure. No problem."

Dad set his fork down. "You asked your father?"

She talked through a bite of burger. "He won't mind."

"Let's just make sure," Dad said. Since it was beginning to get dark he made me walk her to the *Martina*—there was a whole dangerous ten feet between it and the *Loveboat*.

"You wait here," she said. So I stood around, slapping mosquitoes, while she climbed aboard. She slid the hatch, but didn't open the little door. Instead she stood with her legs against it and stuck her head through the hatch. "Captain? I'm going over to the brother's houseboat to decorate a tree, okay?"

"Fine," said a voice from inside the boat. "I'll be across the way with a couple of colleagues. Don't wait up."

"Where's across the way?" I asked as she hopped back down to the dock.

"Over there, across the creek."

The railings of the outdoor bar at Pirate's Bay Resort were lit with strings of Christmas lights. So were the tuna towers of the fishing boats docked in the resort's marina. *Tap, tap, tap.* A finger rapped against a microphone. "Testing, one, two, three."

Someone strummed a chord. "All rightee then, have all of you been good boys and girls? It is the eve of the eve of Christmas, you know." The boys and girls were all adults, sitting at outdoor tables, drinking. "Naughty or nice, this song's for each and every one of you." The voice faded in and out as it drifted across the water. Then the band began to play "Jingle Bell Rock." Loud.

Back inside the houseboat, Dad was swinging Mom in an oldie goldie dance move. Mica tried to get me to dance with her.

"He has three left feet," said Cody, and he launched himself into Mica. While the two of them imitated my parents, I got out of the way. Standing around made me think about the Christmas dance at Monroe Middle.

We all rode over together—me, Clay, Justin, and Leroy. Leroy hung out at the refreshment table, talking to Jemmie. The rest of us hugged the wall. "Ooh, that Jessica wants me," Clay whispered, looking across the room at the girls. "She wants me bad."

"Wants you?" Justin's voice came out of the dark. "Clay, you're deluded."

"Am not. Man, I'm hot tonight. Whaddya say we make a move?" But the three of us stayed put, backs against the wall.

On the first girl's choice Trina made a beeline for me, Cass a little behind her. "Ben?" Trina draped her arms over my neck. I reached up and took one of her hands. I wasn't going to dance wraparound with Trina Boyd, not in front of Cass.

Cass grabbed Justin by his top button and led him a few feet away from the wall. Justin rocked from foot to foot—his idea of dancing. Cass and I watched each other over our partner's shoulders. Clay held up the wall.

When the music across the creek ended, Dad thanked Mom for the dance. "Any time," she said, and she tugged his ponytail. Then she opened the box that held all the Christmas ornaments except the paper cranes.

"This is the first year we'll be able to put these all up since I-don't-remember-when," Dad teased.

Cody hung ornaments any old place. But Mica was taking the matter of ornament distribution seriously. Each time Cody went after another one, she'd take off the one he'd just hung and move it to a different spot. He didn't catch on until she moved the stuffed Santa. "Who moved Santa?"

"I think you put up a different one," she lied.

"Did not. There's only one Santa like this. Ben's girlfriend, Cass, gave it to him."

Mica poked me with a wooden candy cane. "Girlfriend?"

"She's a girl and she's a friend," I said. "Two words. Girl. Friend."

Mica hung the wooden candy cane. "Tell the truth, Cody. Is Cass a girl who's a friend, or is she a girlfriend?"

The boat got real quiet. I knew that Mom and Dad had been wondering too. "At your age," they'd hinted, "you're probably beginning to notice girls." Like there was a certain age when you got struck with this new idea: hey, there's a difference between us and them.

"I dunno." Cody threw up his hands. "One word? Two words? I can't even spell girlfriend."

Mica glanced at herself in a silver ball. "What does Cass look like?"

"She's mostly all freckles," Cody said.

"But is she pretty?"

"Pretty?" Cody repeated, thinking it over. I was about to open my mouth, because if someone else got there first it would be to say that Cass had this knockout older sister. "Yes," he said. "She's pretty. If you like freckles."

"I have a couple," Mica said, lifting her bangs. "See, Ben?"

I turned to Mom. "Where'd you put that bag of cranes?"

"Let's hang them at the tips of the branches," Mica said when Mom brought the cranes out. "We'll let the breeze in. That way they can fly." And she ran around the boat opening more windows.

"Gorgeous," she said, as the cranes turned in the breeze.

"As gorgeous as your twelve-foot trees with a million lights?" Cody asked.

Mica sighed. "Gorgeouser."

Even with all the windows open, it was still pretty warm. "How about the traditional hot chocolate?" Dad said. Mom doesn't buy it any other time of year and he didn't want to miss out.

We sat at the dinette, watching the little marshmallows melt while we waited for the hot chocolate to cool down. It seemed strange to be sweating on the eve of the eve of Christmas.

Dad pushed his empty mug back and stretched. "Well, Mica, it's time for these boys to go to bed." That meant he was ready to turn in himself. "Bet your father's wondering where you are."

Mica wore a chocolate mustache. "Oh, he's probably not home yet. He's across the creek meeting with colleagues."

"You'll be aboard the sailboat all by yourself?"

"No problem." She licked her lips. "It's not like I need someone to tuck me in."

Once again my father had me walk Mica to the *Martina*. "See you Christmas Eve," she said. She climbed aboard and trotted across the deck. I heard the hatch slide open, then shut.

My father was standing on the porch of the houseboat watching the crowd across the creek.

We heard a shout from the outdoor bar. "Hey, hey, if it isn't Mr. Science. How ya been, pal?"

And Mica's dad shouted back, "Hey, Pirate. Hey, Pistol. Mind if I join you two gentlemen for a drink?"

"Mr. Science needs to say adios to his 'colleagues' and get home to his little girl," my father said.

"Relax, Dad. All she's going to do is sleep. Even you and Mom don't hover over us when we sleep." I held the door for him. "You coming?"

"Think I'll sit up a while and watch the water."

And wait for Mr. Science, I thought.

I don't know how long I had been asleep when the hum of a small motor woke me up. It cut out somewhere up by the store. Then I heard singing, "Jingle bell time, what a swell time..." The person kept singing the same line over and over. "Bell time...swell time..."

Thunk, thunk, thunk. Wheels ticked across the uneven boards of the dock.

"Evening, Dr. Delano." Dad's voice.

There was a long pause. "Good evening to you, too."

I waited for the sound of the houseboat door opening. I thought, come on, Dad, you've done your job. But he wouldn't let it rest. "Thanks for letting your daughter help us decorate the tree," he said. "My boy walked her back. We were kind of concerned about sending her home to an empty boat."

Not me, I thought. I wasn't concerned.

"Yes...well. I was gone a little longer than I...um...trying to arrange things. I rarely go off... But it is safe here...very safe. Thanks for keeping an eye, but it was entirely unnecessary."

I agreed with Dr. Delano. Mica was doing some unsupervised sleeping, so what? Okay, Dad, I thought. You gave your speech, now come to bed.

Dr. Delano swore loudly, then complained, "What's the matter with this lock?"

"Here, give me the key." I felt the houseboat list as Dad stepped off. "How much did you have to drink?"

"Two beers," Dr. Delano replied. "Three at most."

"What would your little girl do if something happened to you?"

Dad needed to back off. The man had had a couple of beers, big deal.

Dad isn't a subtle guy, he says it himself, but he must've realized he'd gone a little far. He changed gears. "Mica says you teach marine biology at Caloosa Lodge."

"Teach? Please. I baby-sit. I keep kids from putting jellyfish down each other's backs or using sea cucumbers as water pistols."

"Kids," said Dad, and he laughed. "Say, I bet you have a couple days off for Christmas."

"Yes, thank God."

"Good. I'm taking my boys out oceanside in the morning.

Thought we'd fish a little, maybe snorkel the patches. We'd like it if you and Mica would come along."

Good news/bad news, I thought, lying on my back. Good: we're going out on the ocean. Bad: Mica will be tagging along.

Hopefully Dr. Delano would be too insulted to accept. There was a long silence, then he said, "We'd be pleased to join you." I noticed that a little of the daytime dignity had crept back into his voice. "Thank you for thinking of us."

"All right!" Even inside the boat I heard the slap Dad landed on Dr. Delano's back. "Whoa, buddy! Didn't mean to knock you over! See you in the mornin' then. Bright and early."

chapter fourteen

SNORKELING
WITH JACQUES

"He has a headache," Mica announced as she walked into the marina store. "He says to go without him."

"Plenty of time," Dad said, wiping the dust off a shelf in the spaces between cans of motor oil. "We'll wait for him."

"Wait?" Cody had just wrangled Mom into letting him have a bag of chips because it was Christmas Eve, and because we were going on a voyage, and because, he said, he hadn't had a chip since he was three years old—which was a fat lie. He hugged the bag he wasn't allowed to open until we were out on the water. "But we're ready to go now!"

I was with Cody on this one. The loaded cooler was already aboard our uncle's powerboat, the *Lazy Afternoon*. Mom, who wasn't going because she had a few last-minute things to do for Christmas, had greased us with so much number 30 sunblock it was making us sweat. We were beyond ready.

"Really," Mica said. "We should go. His headaches take a while."

Dad stopped swishing the dust rag around. "How are you at snorkeling, Mica?"

She rolled her eyes. "I've only been doing it since I was like, four years old."

"You think you could teach these guys?"

"*These* two?" She twisted the end of the French braid around her finger as she looked Cody and me over.

"I know they're not much to work with," Dad said. "But could you give it a try?"

"Sure. Okay. No guarantees, though."

He gave us the presents our aunt and uncle had left, two packages each. Cody tore the paper on the bigger one. "Flippers!" He put his on and slapped around the room.

The smaller packages were masks. On the boxes were pictures of Jacques Cousteau, "inventor of the Aqua-Lung, father of modern diving." I took it as a good sign. Jacques wouldn't steer a kid toward a bad mask.

Mica grabbed mine and ran her fingers along the rubbery edge, double-checking Jacques. She held it up to her face, inhaled, and the mask stayed in place. "They don't seem like leakers." Green eyes looked at me through the oval glass. "Unless there's something strange about your faces."

"What could be strange about our faces?" Cody asked.

"Like if they dipped in funny, or you had beards."

"Beards?" Cody laughed. "We're kids. We don't have beards!" He grabbed his stomach he was laughing so hard.

"Flippers on the dock," Mica ordered. "We'll get to them later." She waded into the shallow water and knelt down. "Now, do everything I do." She sloshed the mask she'd gotten off the Martina around in the water. It didn't seem like there was much to snorkeling: slap the mask and flippers on and go. Mica was turning it into a hundred-step process.

"I want to do the flippers *now*," Cody whined. The Jacques Cousteau tag still hung on his mask, for luck, he said. The tag was getting soggy as the mask in his hands filled with saltwater. "Flippers," he repeated.

"Masks first," she said. "Flippers are the hard part. Now, watch carefully." She poured the water out of her mask and spat in it.

"Yuck!" wailed Cody. "I'm not spitting on my Christmas present."

"Got to." As Mica rubbed the spit around with one finger the glass made a squeaky sound.

"That's the grossest thing I've ever seen outside of the school cafeteria," I said.

"Just do it." She worked the spit all the way out to the edges.

Cody sucked up a gob and unloaded it in his new mask.

"So, why are we doing this?" I asked as the two of them played around with their spit. "Just do it," might be good enough for Cody, but I wanted to know why. If it was for luck or something she could forget it.

"Spit keeps your mask from fogging." *Squeak, squeak.* "If you want your mask to fog, don't do it."

Fogging. Okay, I thought. Sorry about this, Jacques.

Once we had the spit spread around, Mica pushed her bangs back. "Now, get all the hair off your forehead. If there's hair under your mask, you'll flood."

"I don't want to flood," said Cody, trying to hold his hair back and do the mask at the same time.

"I got it." I pushed his hair back like I was taking his temperature.

"Put the mask in the right place first, *then* do the strap," Mica advised.

I put his mask where I thought it should go, then slid the strap down. Cody blinked behind the glass. "There you go," I said. "All set. Go swim like Jacques."

Mica gripped the front of the mask and tugged. "Too loose." She crawled around behind him. One brown knee appeared on either side of him. *Click, click, click.*

My brother's eyes bugged. "Too tight!" he gasped. *Click.* Mica tightened it another notch. A hand reached around and jerked on the mask. This time when the mask moved, Cody's head went with it. "I feel like I have a giant sucker on my face," he complained. "I don't have any blood going to my brain."

I put on my own giant sucker mask and pulled the strap until the blood quit going to my brain too. I held my hands up to fend Mica off. "Hey, it's good," I said, but Mica had to make sure. She about pulled me over.

"Now for the snorkel," she said, and she reached for the long tube that dangled off the strap on the left side of her mask. "Put the mouthpiece between your teeth and bite down. This floppy rubber part goes inside your lips." She bit down on her snorkel and arranged her lips. We did the same. "Follow me," she said through clenched teeth, her voice reverberating in the hollow tube.

Tasting the plasticky flavor of our snorkels, me and my brother followed Mica under the dock. When we stood waist deep in the canal she lay down and floated, mask in the water. I could hear her breathing through her snorkel. She stood back up. "See?" she said. "Easy cheesy." She lay down again and kicked slowly away from the dock.

"Give it a try, Cody," I said, my voice echoing too.

Luckily I had talked Mica into letting my brother wear his wings. It would be tough to learn to snorkel and swim at the same time. With the wings, he floated just fine. He was bobbing facedown when Mica swam back and grabbed his hand.

I took a deep breath and submerged my mask too. Warm water lapped at my ears. The first thing I saw, just below the surface, was a school of glass minnows. Seen from the dock, glass minnows are a dull, speckled gray like pebbles, but with light behind them, they look like swimming neon lights. A rippling shimmer of blue runs down their sides. Above them, the underside of the water was a shiny silver mirror. My arms were silver too. Tiny air bubbles clung to the hairs. I brushed a hand over an arm and the bubbles shivered off.

Under the water was a whole different, fantastic world. The plants on the bottom swayed as if a wind was blowing. A jellyfish drifted by like a falling parachute. I heard a loud rushing sound. It took a second to realize it was my own breathing.

Suddenly, my heart clenched. A pair of giant fish was coming right at me! Then I recognized the black and yellow stripes. It was only a couple of sergeant majors, up close. One came right to the glass. I thought it was looking at me, but then it kissed the front of the mask, trying to feed maybe. It didn't seem to see me as anything different from a piling in the water until I moved. Then it darted away.

Mica's legs churned as she swam toward the houseboat, dragging Cody. Their skin—even Mica's—looked pale and greenish. The Jacques Cousteau tag trailed beside my brother's ear. When Cody reached out to touch the ruby red sponges that covered a mooring rope, Mica pulled his hand back and shook her head. Maybe he'd hurt them if he touched them. Maybe they'd hurt him.

I caught up, and we paddled along the side of the houseboat, looking underneath. Snappers and one long, needley barracuda with an underslung jaw full of teeth hung in the shade.

After a while Mica let us try our flippers, but she was right, they were hard to use. The flipper blades and my feet were always at the opposite end of the stroke, foot going one way, flipper going the other. My ankles burned. Disgusted, I threw them on the dock. Cody's were there already.

Mica tried to teach us to dive. "Blow a little air out to keep your snorkels from filling." Cody took off his wings and went bottoms-up in three feet of water. He came up coughing. I did okay.

By the time we crawled back under the dock we were all pretty tired. Mica spat out her snorkel. "Okay, brothers," she said. "You two are ready for the true sea."

"Really?" Cody asked.

"Well, more or less."

We broke the suction between the masks and our faces. *Pop, pop, pop.* Cody pointed and gave a hiccupy laugh. "You look like your face is gonna fold in half, Ben."

"Like origami," Mica added.

I laughed. "Oh, yeah? You guys have origami faces too." Our sucker masks had left deep grooves.

Cody put his knee on the dock. "Ow!" he said, as he climbed out. "It's hot." While he hopped around we got out too. Mica turned on the spigot that was strapped to a piling. Rushing to cool his feet, Cody picked up the hose.

Mica slapped it out of his hand. "The water that's been sitting in the hose is boiling." She sprayed the dock for a full minute before testing it on her foot. Then she held the hose over her own head, taking the first turn. Her old blue swimsuit collected water at the butt. When she held the hose over Cody the end of her French braid dripped like a spout.

I was turning the water off when I heard the hatch on the *Martina* slide. Dr. Delano's arms emerged, then his head, then his shoulders. He blinked like a bear coming out of hibernation. "Brutal," he said. He pinched the bridge of his nose and closed his eyes.

Mica flung down the hose. "Good morning, Captain," she sang out. "We waited for you!"

"Mercy," he groaned. "Mica, I couldn't possibly—"

But Mica smattered the dock with dancing footprints. "We can go now!" she sang out as she trotted down the dock. "Ready, Mr. Floyd! The Captain's up."

chapter fifteen

THE TRUE SEA

D r. Delano stumbled off the *Martina* in cutoff jeans, a faded T-shirt, and his pith helmet. Coffee sloshed out of the mug in his hand.

"Come on, Captain!" Mica leapt from the dock to the powerboat to join Cody and me. "Everybody's waiting for you. The gear's already aboard."

"Mornin'," Dad boomed. "Glad you could join us."

Dr. Delano took tiny, shuffling steps, as if his feet hurt. "Wouldn't have missed it for the world," he groaned, and stepped down into the boat. He had to catch himself on the edge of the windshield to keep from falling over. The rest of the coffee spilled. He stared gloomily into his empty cup, then down at the coffee on the deck. "You'll have to excuse me." He sighed loudly and rubbed his eyes. "I get terrible migraines."

"Some fresh sea air will do you good, sir!" Mica pushed him into the captain's chair. Dr. Delano didn't seem up to piloting a boat. One look at Dad and I knew it wasn't going to happen, even though all he said was, "You three kids can share the bench seat up front." As he climbed back to the dock to get the lines we squeezed onto the seat in front of the console.

Dad was still taking the first knot out of the bowline when Cody tore into the bag of chips and stuffed his mouth. "Wan' some?" he asked Mica, spraying her with bits of chip.

Dad cast off the stern line then hopped in and slid between Mica's dad and the wheel. He turned the key in the ignition. The *Lazy Afternoon* started right up. "Good girl," he said, and patted the dashboard. As he eased the throttle forward the water behind the boat churned, and we pulled away from the dock.

Idling down the canal, I felt the deep thrum of the twin diesels through the soles of my feet. I smelled exhaust. The *Martina* and the houseboat rolled on our wake as we passed. They tugged at their lines like they wanted to break free.

Mica pointed to the flag at the Coast Guard station. "Straight down," she called back to her father. "It'll be nice and calm."

"Good," he answered.

With Dr. Delano slumped in the captain's chair, Dad had to stand at the wheel. From where I sat, it looked as if Dad was carrying Mica's father on his back.

"Get the outriggers, Ben," Dad called.

In a car I could've put my hand on anything he named, but this was a boat. I had no idea what an outrigger was.

"Got 'em." Mica jumped up. She loosened a thumbscrew and dropped one of the two whiplike poles that rose twelve feet above the gunwales of the powerboat. I beat her to the second one. Outriggers down, we passed under the bridge. The glug of the engines boomed off the concrete overpass.

Dad followed the channel. The sand flats on either side were high and dry. Mica hooked her heels over the edge of the seat and wrapped her arms around her shins. "Tide's low," she called to her father.

"It will be in half an hour," he answered. I caught a glimpse of him when Dad leaned to the side. His eyes were closed.

"Look, Cody. That's a cormorant." Mica pointed out a bird that sat on a channel marker. "He's drying his wings."

The sea that stretched ahead of us was smooth and hazy with a dull shine, like oil, and about the same color as the sky. The horizon looked like a faint pencil line someone had tried to erase. For a second I imagined we were off St. Marks in the skiff, going after redfish. But everything was bigger here: the boat, the voice of the engine as we left the channel—and the fish I planned to catch.

"Grab your socks!" Dad yelled, and he jammed the throttle forward all the way. Instantly, the pitch of the engine went from a low gurgle to a deep roar and the bow of the *Lazy Afternoon* reared up. Chips blew out of Cody's hand. When he complained, the wind whipped the words right out of his mouth. Up on plane, we skimmed, barely touching water, flying between sky and sea.

Dad's ponytail whipped. He wore a big grin. Dad likes going fast. He likes making noise. Eyes still shut, Mica's father lifted his pith helmet and let the wind blow his thin hair around. The shore behind us dissolved in a bright haze.

I wanted to stand up and lean into the wind that pushed against my chest, catch it full force. I wanted to holler.

Small fish darted beside the boat, airborne for a hundred feet before stabbing back into the waves. Mica cupped her hands around her mouth. "Flying fish," she shouted.

"Really?" I shouted back. "I thought they were only in cartoons."

We cut through the air until my skin tingled. If I turned my head just right, the wind was strong enough to make my lips flap. Our T-shirts were glued to our chest in front, but puffed out fat behind us.

We'd been running a while when a small tower appeared on the horizon. It looked like something I could have made with my old Erector set. I pointed. "Hens and Chickens," Mica yelled in my ear.

I turned to Cody and shouted. "Hens and Chickens." But he was still chowing down on potato chips, head half in the bag.

Gradually, the toy tower got bigger. "We're crossing Hawks Channel," she said. "It's deeper here."

"Hawks Channel," I shouted at Cody.

As the tower grew to life-size, I noticed white dots on the water around it. "What're those?"

"Buoys. They mark lobster traps. The bottom's shallowing up." The dark water was getting lighter, more like the green glass in the thick part of a Coke bottle.

Dad throttled back and the hull settled. Ripples washed out as we displaced more water. "Hens and Chickens," Dad said. We'd quit flying.

"How'd you know how to find it?" I asked.

"Uncle Bert used to take us to Hens and Chickens when I was a kid. It's like falling off a bicycle. You never forget how to do it."

Cody quit grazing. "I don't see any chickens."

Dr. Delano finally opened his eyes. "Hens and Chickens is the name of this particular patch reef," he said. "It's inshore of the true reef, but still interesting." Dad hitched his pants, all set to cowboy up to the bow and drop anchor.

Dr. Delano put a hand on his arm. "I'll get the anchor." He set the pith helmet back on his head and stood. Mica reached out to steady him as he passed. Somehow he made it to the bow without falling overboard. He knelt and shoved the anchor partway under the rail, then watched the bottom glide by.

"What's he waiting for?" Cody asked.

"Sand," Mica said. "Stupid boaters drop their anchors in the coral. He's looking for a sand patch so we can anchor up without doing damage."

The anchor went overboard with a splash. "Idle it in neutral." Dr. Delano held up a hand. "Good. All right, let the wind carry us back." He let out more line. "That's it, that's it." We drifted back until we felt the anchor bite. "Stop." He held up one hand. "Cut the engine. Let's see if it holds."

I had stopped noticing how loud the engine was until it quit. In the silence the *Lazy Afternoon* swung slowly on its anchor rope. I licked my finger and held it up, but I didn't feel any wind.

"Current," Mica said.

The current turned us ninety degrees and then the boat stopped. "Fine," said Dr. Delano. He lifted his pith helmet and set it on the bow, brim up like a bowl. He peeled his T-shirt off, folded it carefully, and put it in the hat. Like his leg, the left side of his chest was scarred with a road map of lines.

"Look at those—Ow!" Cody rubbed his thigh. "Why'd you go and pinch me, Ben?"

"Get up, you guys," Mica ordered. We stood, and she opened the bench seat to unpack the snorkel gear. As soon as he got his, Dr. Delano did a back roll over the bow rail. With one arm around the anchor rope he did the spitting thing, then positioned his mask. He pulled the strap over his head—and he was gone. The rest of us watched over the side. Using his powerful arms he flew through the clear water.

The rest of us hung over the transom to slosh our masks in the water. We spat; we rubbed spit. I helped Cody put his mask on. All that was left of the Jacques tag was the string.

Dad slid a wing on Cody's arm and blew it up.

"What about Ben?" Cody whined.

Dad slipped on the second wing. "Ben can swim." Once the wings were done, Dad picked up his own mask. He pulled his ponytail through so it would hang over the strap, and slapped the mask on. He stood on the transom a while watching Dr. Delano swim circles around something that looked like a brain.

Mica dove. When she reached her dad, she wrapped her arms around his neck. He fanned a little sediment away with one hand and pointed to the giant brain. A ribbon of small fish swam between us and the divers.

"Geronimo!" Dad shouted. He pulled his knees up and jumped. Me and Cody got drenched. Every fish for five miles spooked. Compared to Mica's dad he swam like a giant bug that had accidentally fallen in.

With Mica still attached, Dr. Delano surfaced. Their hair was smoothed back. They looked as sleek as a pair of dolphins. Each of them took a quick breath and dove again, swimming away from the turbulence that surrounded Dad.

I snapped the elastic waist of Cody's trunks. "Let's go, bro."

I took a few free dives, and got pretty close to the giant brain. With practice, I thought, I could get good at this. Most of the time I hung on the surface with Cody, watching Mica and her dad. They looked as if they were in their natural element.

They were swimming for the bottom when Cody called, "Ben?" I didn't lift my mask out of the water. He was obviously alive and breathing. "Ben!"

"What?" Through the water pouring down the front of my mask I saw Cody, going up and down, clinging to the anchor rope.

"I don't feel so good," he said.

"What'd you expect, bud? You ate a whole bag of chips."

"It's not the chips. It's the sloshing."

The sea was calm, but even though there were no breaking waves, plenty of long, slow swells lifted the powerboat then dropped it with a slap. Cody rose and fell, rose and fell, rose and... I was beginning to feel sick just watching him when he puked.

"Oh, man..." I kicked away from him as chips drifted toward me.

"I couldn't help it!" he said as the boat lifted him up again.

The Delanos surfaced with Dad right behind them.

Seeing the patch of chips on the water, they all eyed Cody and me. Mica spat out her snorkel. "Nice," she said, hanging off her father's back. "The brothers shot their cookies."

"Hey," I said. "Don't look at me!"

"Poor little guy." Dad plowed right through the chips to get to my brother. "He always has been an easy-barfer."

"*Da-aad!*" Now Cody was sick *and* embarrassed.

The sinking chips attracted small fish. "Better than chum," Mica said.

Cody's face was the color of lettuce. "I want to go home," he blubbered.

Dr. Delano spat out his snorkel and pushed his mask up. "Lots of people feel queasy in this kind of sea," he said. "I used to get so sick I almost switched fields, but believe me, Cody, you can get used to it."

"I don't wanna get used to it!" Cody looked like he was about to barf again.

"Try watching the horizon."

In about half a second Cody moaned, "It's not working."

Dr. Delano gently unhooked Mica's arms from around his neck. "Let me see what I can do for this young man, Mica." He put his mask back on and held out his hands. "Come on, Cody. Swim to me."

"I can't let go of the rope."

"Trust me. I won't let you sink."

Cody flailed across the gap. Dr. Delano caught him under the stomach and held him in his arms. "Now, put your snorkel in. Just relax, I've got you." Cody bit down on the snorkel. "Now, I want you to put your mask in the water and float face down. There you go. Can you hear what I'm saying, Cody?" The snorkel bobbed. "Good."

As he spoke, Dr. Delano gradually lowered his arms until Cody was floating on his own. "Give me your hand. I'll take you on a guided tour." I grabbed ahold of Cody's other hand and put my mask in the water too. In a second I felt Mica take my free hand—a weird development. Swimming with one arm, Dr. Delano towed the three of us along.

Dr. Delano would submerge his mask, take a quick look, then come back up to describe what he'd seen. "We're right over a bed of sea fans. The Latin name is *Gorgonia* and they're animals. Divers collect and dry them. Some even spray-paint them." His laugh wasn't really a laugh. "Stupid," he said, meaning the people who spray-painted sea fans, I guess.

The lavender sea fans waved in the current. They could never be as pretty as that dried stiff and painted. Stupid, I thought—and I did mean the people.

"Beside the *Gorgonia* you'll see brain coral, then elkhorn coral. The elkhorn likes to grow on the windward side of the reef. Those white scratches are where something hit it—an anchor line perhaps, or the edge of a flipper."

Suddenly, a large, dark phantom passed between us and the reef. It fanned its broad, flat wings. "A spotted eagle ray!" Dr. Delano's voice was excited. "What a big beauty! I'll bet she's eight feet long."

I felt Mica let go. She dove, and put one hand on either side of the eagle ray's head. I dove right behind her and grabbed her ankles. I felt the power of the ray as it towed us along. We both came up grinning.

"Jacks at one o'clock," said Dr. Delano, and we put our masks underwater again. A school of jacks was swimming toward us fast, heads swinging side to side. They looked tough with their blunt, hatchet faces and forked tails. Man, I thought, I'd love to hook into one of those.

"Oh!" Dr. Delano sounded surprised. "Now how did I miss that? Eyes down everyone. Look." We hadn't seen the big fish lying on the bottom because it was drab and its head was under a ledge of coral. "That's a nurse shark," he said. "See the sickle tail?" My brother squeezed my hand so hard the bones inside almost touched each other.

"How big do you think that sucker is?" I heard Dad ask.

"Twelve feet or better."

Cody tore his hand out of mine. His flipper jabbed me in the side. The water churned.

"Cody, you're perfectly safe," Dr. Delano called. "I assure you, that shark is not interested in you."

"He's seen *Jaws,*" I said as Cody tried to climb the rope.

"Damn that movie," Dr. Delano muttered. "That wasn't a shark. It was a machine. The number of people killed by sharks is miniscule compared to the millions of sharks killed by people."

But Cody still had nightmares about that great white, so when he couldn't get up the rope he thrashed his way to the stern. He scraped his chest, but managed to haul himself up and over the transom.

I just happened to look down. I think I was the only one who saw the shark swim away, swinging its long sickle tail.

chapter sixteen

THAT CASS PERSON

The three of us lay on the bow, watching the clouds boil up from the horizon. "I see a dog," my brother said.

"No," Mica said. "A dragon."

"Dog," Cody insisted. "It has a collar, see?"

We ate the sandwiches Mom had packed—except for Cody. He drank a bottle of water, then fell asleep. Dr. Delano sat in the captain's chair again. He put his empty sandwich bag in one of his pockets and cocked his pith helmet so it shaded his eyes. He crossed his arms, tucked his hands in his armpits, and fell asleep too.

I was lying there, eyes shut, feeling the sun on my face, when I heard the click of a reel. "Let's see what we got here," said Dad, casting a line out over the patch reef. *All right!* It was finally time to pick up a rod. But when I opened my eyes, Mica was sitting cross-legged, staring down at me. "What're you looking at?" I asked.

"Nothing."

I pushed up on my elbows. I could see Dad through the windshield, reeling in slow. Every now and then he jerked the rod to catch the eye of anything that happened to be down there. "Think I'll get a line wet," I said.

A hand landed smack in the middle of my bare chest. "Come on, Ben, talk to me. Tell me about that Cass person."

I'd been dying to fish and now was my chance, but thanks to Mom, I was too polite to push a girl. "Two minutes," I said, "And only if you get your hand off me."

"Come on, come on, take it," Dad coaxed softly. Something was tapping at his bait.

"So, tell me. What about Cass?" said Mica.

I shot for the quick version. "We were babies together." Blah, blah, blah. I heard Dad cast again. Whatever had been checking out his bait had lost interest.

Blah, blah, blah. "We always went to the same schools."

Just because Dad wasn't having any luck didn't mean I wouldn't. But Mica kept asking questions, daisy-chaining the story out. I could see my spinning rod in the rod holder. I could practically feel the grip in my hand.

Time to cut the story short.

I was telling her about Cass winning races—about to say The End and grab my rod—when Dad let out a yelp. I turned in time to see his rod bend double, the tip plunging right into the water.

"Way to go, Dad!" We were used to catching speckled perch and bream on Lake Talquin or trout and reds in the Gulf—decent-sized fish, but nothing that could bend a rod like that. I jumped up and hopped down into the back of the boat.

"Bet I could outrun that girl," said Mica.

"What?" The rod was in my hand, but that caught my attention. "Outrun Cass? Dream on."

Dad scrambled up on the transom. He held the rod way out, trying to keep the fish from wrapping the line around the rudder. "Holy guacamole!" he shouted as the fish made a run straight under the boat.

"Save one for me, Dad!"

"Why couldn't I beat her?" Mica pestered. "I'm pretty fast."

I threw open the lid on the live well. "She's not *pretty* fast, she's *super* fast. Cass has medals from State."

Mica knelt on the bow with her hands on the top of the windshield. "Bet I could beat her if I really tried."

"Whatever." I grabbed a shrimp. A nice big one.

"Bet I've been more places than she has."

Dad let out a yell. "Baby, oh baby! Here she comes!" Still holding the rod, he leaned over the side and netted the fish he'd been fighting. "Mutton snapper," he said, lifting the dripping net. "I bet it weighs seven, eight pounds easy." The fish he lifted out of the net was reddish-pink with a spot near the tail, a beauty.

"Nice one, Dad." I wanted one just like it—but a little bigger.

"Christmas Eve dinner!" Dad dropped the fish in the cooler of ice. "Let's go folks. Time to kiss the cook!"

"But Dad..." I held the shrimp in one hand, the hook in the other.

"You had your chance, bud. You were too busy flirting with Mica."

"Don't make me gag, Dad." I tossed the shrimp back in the live well.

I didn't get in one cast. Not one. I wanted to kill Mica.

Mom stuffed Dad's mutton snapper like a turkey. She's a vegetarian, but she still eats fish. The men in the Floyd family don't ask what the difference between a fish life and a cow life is. If we did, seafood might join fried chicken and cheeseburgers on the forbidden food list. And we like seafood—it's all we have left.

Mica and her father came over for dinner. The six of us crowded the small dinette. I had to share one bench with Mica and Cody. Mom and Dad had the other one. Dr. Delano pulled a chair up to the free end. He didn't eat much but he told great stories. He talked about solving the mystery of why sea grass beds were suddenly dying. And he told about being caught in a tropical storm aboard the *Martina*. "Halfway through the night, the mast snapped," he said. "Remember that, Mica?"

Mica shivered. "It was the worst!"

And then there were the islands. Palm islands and desert islands and islands with springs of bubbling fresh water. "Some islands are so small they don't rate a dot on the map," he said. "Mica names those herself."

"What kind of names do you give 'em?" Cody asked.

Mica sucked butter off her fingers while she thought. Although her father's manners were perfect, hers were terrible. Nonexistent. "It depends on what they look like," she said, reaching in front of me to grab a roll.

"Tell me some of them," Cody begged. Cody is always naming things. When he was little he named his shoes Bert and Ernie. Bert was the right one. Ernie was the left.

"Sleeping Dog, Lobster Tail, Fisheye."

Dr. Delano leaned toward Mica and lowered his voice. "Tell them about Big Suck."

Big Suck—now there was a name the guys could appreciate.

Mica grinned. "Big Suck was an island with a quicksand bog in the middle. It sucked me down and almost swallowed me."

I poked my brother and whispered, "Ya think you could you open your eyes a little wider?" I was impressed too, but I remembered the Rocky DeGarza creed, Attitude. I buttered my roll and looked bored. "So, what did you do?"

"First, I stopped struggling. That's the worst thing you can do."

Cody nodded like he was making a mental note for the next time he was in quicksand.

"Then I lay back and floated. You can do that if you hold really still. After a while my father found me, but I could have died."

"No lie?" Cody asked.

"No lie," confirmed Dr. Delano.

I stabbed a piece of boiled potato with my fork. When it came to danger, all I had to brag about was the time I got nailed by the Winthrop's beagle. Me and Cass were crawling under hedges playing spies when I stuck my head out. I still have a scar by my eye, but, big deal. It was a stupid mistake and I was only seven when it happened.

The years between seven and thirteen and a half have been a long, dry spell in the danger department.

I wanted the stories to go on and on. Normally, Cody would too, but instead he kept fake-yawning and saying, "Time for bed, you guys. Time for bed." Maybe he was afraid that Santa would find us awake and water-ski right by without leaving presents.

As soon as Mica and her father left, Cody said, "Get the sign out, Mom." He turned to me. "We made a sign while you and Dad were out fixing the truck."

Cody and Mom's sign said Dear Santa, Cody and Ben are here. "Go ahead," Mom urged. "Tape it to the porch rail." She began washing the dishes.

Cody stared at the sign. "We need to add Mica."

"There isn't a whole lot of room," I said. I knew there were no presents for Mica under the cot in the ice-cream truck.

"We can squish it in, can't we, Mom?"

Mom dried her hands on a towel and took a marker out of a drawer by the sink.

"Mom?" I said. "Mica's been off his list a while. Santa probably doesn't have anything in his bag for her."

"He'll have something," she said. The marker squeaked across the paper. "It's a big bag."

chapter seventeen

CASS'S GIFT

Ben?" Cody's voice came out of the dark. "You awake?"
"Yeah, I'm awake." Rain fell on the houseboat roof.
"Santa's gonna get soaked," he said.

"He'll be waterskiing, remember? What's a little more water?"

"What about the presents?"

"The bag's waterproof, Cody."

"Oh." I heard him roll over in the bunk across the room. "That's good." His voice sounded drifty. In a minute he began to snore.

The rain was light for a while, like squirrels running across the roof back home. I wondered if it was raining in Tallahassee too. Had Cass put my present under the tree? And if she had, was there any chance her father would miss seeing her open it? And how was I going to open the one from her without everyone here seeing it—just in case it was something personal?

Not that I thought it was.

I mean, it probably wasn't.

It definitely wasn't.

But maybe...

It rained harder. The houseboat rocked as the wind blew. I rolled onto my stomach.

The next time I woke up it was Christmas morning—but barely. My shorts were on the floor by the bed where I'd dropped them. I reached out and fished them up, then stood. I had just put a foot through a leg hole when the boat moved. Hopping around, I crashed my shin on the edge of the bunk.

Cody snorted. I leaned against the mirror and listened until he rolled over and went back to breathing slow.

I put on a clean T-shirt, then slid my hand under the clothes in my suitcase. I felt around until I heard the faint crunch of wrapping paper. Cass's present. I hid the gift under my shirt and snuck out of the room.

Dad and Mom slept on the foldout sofa. The cranes on the Christmas tree turned in the breeze. When Cody saw all the presents spilling out from under the tree, his eyes would be big as two fried eggs.

Covered by Dad's snoring, I opened the door and let myself onto the porch. The floor was cold and wet. There wasn't much light. With their heads down, the pelicans on the pilings up by the store looked like wads of old chewing gum.

Cody's message for Santa was soaked. Mom must've added Mica's name with a different kind of marker. Ours were okay, but hers had bled so bad you couldn't read it anymore. If none of the presents under the tree were for her, I'd tell Cody that was the reason.

For a while I sat in the rocker with Cass's package on my knees, afraid to see what was inside. Excited too. It was definitely time to open the gift. It didn't seem right to rip into it, though, since the Bodines had been so careful to reuse the wrapping paper. I peeled back the tape on one end, slid my present out, and put it in my lap on top of the paper.

"Wow." It was personal all right—and dangerous. Dangerous because her mom would kill Cass when she found out what she'd done. To make my Christmas collage, Cass must've cut up every picture in her mother's albums that showed the two of us together—except for the ones of us as butt-naked babies.

The day we put our handprints in the sidewalk was there. Mrs. Bodine snapped us with our hands squished in the cement. Cass had Band-Aids on both knees.

Cass had written Say Cheese! under a shot of us with our fingers hooked in the corners of our mouths. We were showing off our missing teeth.

The first day of school was there. Cass was sulking because her mom made her wear a dress. My hair stuck up in back, like Cody's does all the time.

There were three Halloweens: doctor and nurse, cat and dog. And dragon. I was the tail, Cass was the head. You can tell if you look at our shoes.

She massacred class pictures to get at the part with both of us in it. In a couple of them she stood behind me. For a while, she was taller.

We wore our mothers' sunglasses at Wakulla Springs. One of Lou's hands was on each of our shoulders. Cass had cut the rest of her sister out. We sat on the sawdust floor in the Flying High Circus tent, scared by the clown blowing bubbles at us. Cass even included one of us asleep on the floor in my family's living room all curled up together.

There was only one picture that didn't show the two of us. It was a new one of just her, a glamour shot taken at the mall. Scrawled underneath was "Lou made me do it." The photo shoot was probably Cass's Christmas present from her sister, along with doing her makeup and hair and lending her the fuzzy pink sweater she wore in the picture.

I'd been sneaking up on that shot, looking at the ones of us together, but glancing at it now and then to prepare myself. When I looked at it full on, it was still a shock. Was that really Cass? What had Lou done to her freckles? I could hardly see them, and Cass has so many she calls herself a freckle farm. The whole picture looked kind of misty, like a perfume ad or something. Instead of her usual ponytail, her hair hung around her shoulders. Lou had even gotten the ends to curl.

I was concentrating on her hair and stuff—but there was something else. A few girls in our class, like Patrice Miller and Jennifer

Stanley, wear tight shirts all the time, advertising their new boobs. Everyone knows they have them. But Cass wears big baggy shirts, so it's hard to tell. I figured something was happening under there, but I thought it was like my height—something that wasn't all the way there yet. Lou's sweater showed that Cass was farther along than me. Way farther.

I felt weird staring at her chest. Even with the makeup and different hair, it was still Cass, but the boobs were like these alien creatures. Scary, but definitely interesting. I looked at a couple of the other pictures, then back at her boobs.

I heard a shout. "Mom! Dad! Somebody stole Ben."

Sliding the present back inside, I tore the paper. For the time being, I hid it behind a planter. I didn't want my whole family checking out Cass's boobs.

"Thought you guys were going to sleep 'til New Year's," I said, walking in.

Dad sat up and scratched his belly. "Well, boys, it looks like Santa found us."

"He must've seen the sign." Cody sank down at the edge of the pile of presents. "Can we open?"

Mom held her arms out. "Family hug first!" We all did the piling-on thing.

"Okay," I said when we'd been hugging for about a week. "Enough already. Let's open presents."

Santa gave us the usual mix of fun things and educational things. I got a rock tumbler. Cody got plastic stained glass. "Hey, Ben," Cody said. "Thanks for the yo-yo." We both got scooters. There was a whistling Frisbee for Cody and an NBA regulation basketball for me. Books. A poster of the solar system that glowed in the dark. An ant farm for Cody because he wanted pets and Mom was allergic to fur.

"All right!" I said, tearing the paper off a new spinning rod and reel.

Cody got a rod and reel too, his first.

As he dug through the stacks Cody seemed to be looking for something. Finally, he picked up a box and shouted. "See, Ben, I knew he could do it!" Written on the tag, in Mom's handwriting, was For Mica From Santa. When we'd unwrapped all the presents with our own names on them, there were four left for Mica. Cody squeezed the gifts to his chest. "Let's take them to her."

"They might still be asleep," said Dad.

"On Christmas? Get serious, Dad." Cody headed for the door.

"Want to put some clothes on first?" I asked. He shook his head. "Cody, your PJs have sheep all over them, for crying out loud."

"So?"

"Don't wake them up," Dad warned.

Outside, wind whistled in the *Martina's* rigging. The hardware clanged against the mast. It wasn't exactly raining but there was a fine mist in the air. The sailboat's windows were dark. "Nobody's up, Cody." But the tide was just right for Cody to step from the dock to the *Martina*. In a flash, he was aboard.

"We'll come back later," I said, as small drops stung my face and arms. "You heard Dad. He said don't wake 'em up." I climbed aboard to haul him back to the dock, but he was already knocking. "What're you doing?"

"I'm not knocking loud."

With a hiss, a rainsquall crossed Snake Creek. It swept over the Coast Guard station and the houseboat. It drenched us. "Come on, Cody, let's get outta here!"

Just then the small door below the hatch opened. "Brothers? What're you guys doing here?"

"Bringing presents!" Cody said.

She grabbed Cody by the front of his PJs and pulled him through the door.

Rain was bouncing off my back, so I dove after Cody.

Mica put her finger to her lips and pointed to a narrow door. "The Captain's in the aft cabin." She grabbed me by the shirt and dragged both of us. "I sleep up in the V-berth. Follow me." With one toe, she lifted the blue curtain that hung in the bow. "This is the fo'c'sle," she whispered. "My room."

Mica's room was shaped like a wedge of pie. The walls slanted out. Each had a round porthole for a window. She scrambled up onto the narrow bunk that ran along one wall and slid her legs inside a crumpled sleeping bag. She picked up her pillow and hugged it, eyeing the presents. I noticed that one of her thumbs looked wrinkly and pink, like she'd been sucking it.

Cody and I shared the second bunk with two laundry bags. The words "Clean" and "Dirty" were written on them in marker. It was pretty crowded.

"Are all these people your family?" Cody asked, looking at the dozens of pictures taped to the walls.

Mica took her eyes off the presents for a second. "Friends. Can't you read?"

A computer-printed banner taped above the photos said A Friend in Every Port. In each shot Mica stood beside someone different.

"You sure have a lot of friends." Cody handed her the first gift absentmindedly. "Who's the girl with her arm around your neck?"

Clutching the present, Mica crawled out of the sleeping bag. She read the name off the bottom of the picture. "Oh yeah. Rosalita Asturia."

Rosalita wore a bikini with daisies on it. Mica wore the usual blue swimsuit—although it looked a lot newer in the picture. I was beginning to think it was glued on.

"My father worked with her father on the sea grass project." Mica tore into the package with such force it exploded, spilling shiny fabric. "A swimsuit and cover-up. Matching!" She kicked the sleeping bag to the floor, then laid the cover-up out carefully, smoothing it against the bunk. "Look, guys. It has hibiscus flowers and macaws on it." First she arranged the swimsuit on top of the jacket, then she opened the jacket and put the swimsuit inside so it just peeked out.

"Who's this?" Cody put a finger in the middle of a picture. Mica sat on the back of a motorcycle. Her arms were around a guy with thick black hair and a pack of cigarettes rolled in his T-shirt sleeve. He could have been one of Dad's backyard guys. "Is he your boyfriend?" Cody asked. The *i*'s in Miguel Dominguez were dotted with hearts.

"Miguel was the Captain's student assistant. He was giving me a ride to the dentist. I don't have a boyfriend...yet."

I could tell she was looking at me because it felt like bugs were walking on the back of my neck. "How about this one?" I asked, tapping the nearest photo. In it she was building a sand castle with a couple of kids about Cody's age.

"Ron and Lucy." Mica slipped her arms in the sleeves of the cover-up.

"It says *Roger* and Lucy."

She shrugged. "Ron and Lucy? Roger and Lucy? Who cares? I only hung out with them because there was nobody else around."

Traveling as much as she did, I guess it was potluck. Sometimes she got Miguel, the hunk with the motorcycle. Sometimes she got Roger and Lucy with their little plastic shovels. This week she had the brothers, Ben and Cody, soon to be another picture on the wall.

She stretched a leg across the gap between bunks and prodded a package with her toes. "Is that for me too?"

"This one? Yeah, it is." Cody tossed it over to her. She tore that one open too. Turquoise flip-flops, still tied together, tumbled out and fell on top of the sleeping bag on the floor. Mica fished them up by the plastic tie that held them together. She slid them on, then swung her tied-together feet, watching the flash of blue rubber. She poked one of the remaining two gifts with a turquoise toe. "And this one, who's this one for?"

"You!" said Cody. "They're all for you. Here, catch!"

Mom had loaded a box with girl stuff: hairbrush and hand mirror, barrettes, conditioner, perfume.

Cody squealed, "Gross!" when she sprayed him with perfume. He wiped his arm on the "Clean" laundry bag.

Mica snatched the last package off his lap but opened it slowly, peeling the tape like I had done with Cass's gift. It seemed as if this was all the Christmas she was going to have. I'm not saying that Christmas is only about getting. There's also eating and being with family. But in her case, the food and family part didn't look too promising either. Her father was sleeping in, and her mother was celebrating the holidays on The Continent—which didn't happen to be the same continent Mica was on. I hoped Mom had gotten her something good.

The last package was a stuffed blue bear. Mom was way off. Mica was a tomboy; besides, at eleven, she was too old for stuffed animals.

Mica crushed the blue bear to her chest and smelled the top of its head. "So cute!" I guess that for a girl, even at eleven, a stuffed bear could go either way. When she sprayed the toy with perfume and put a fat barrette on each of its ears, I decided that Mom understood girls way better than I did. "I'm going to name her Floyd after you two brothers," Mica declared.

"It should be Floydette," said Cody, "if it's a girl."

"Floyd," she said, straightening a barrette.

"Who's this?" I asked. It was a blurry picture of a woman with a baby in her lap.

Mica leaned across, holding Floyd by the arm. "Me," she said, tapping the baby with one of Floyd's fuzzy paws. "My mother, the famous ballet dancer." The stuffed bear patted the woman on the head.

"No way!" I blurted out.

Mica stopped clapping Floyd's paws. "No way what?"

"No way your mother's a ballet dancer."

"And why not?"

"Because she's porky," I said. "Mom took us to see Nutcracker once and all the dancers were really skinny. Right, Cody?"

Her lips trembled. "Are you calling my mother fat?"

"Not fat. Just too big to be a ballet dancer."

Mica turned on the faucet. Boom. Instant tears. "You're calling my mother fat!"

"No! I'm calling you a liar!"

"You're saying that's not my mother?" Her voice was getting higher and higher like fireworks going up.

"She may be your mom, but she's no dancer."

"Oh, yes she is! The best! For your information, she makes buckets of money. She meets us in different ports. When she flies in we stay at fancy hotels and eat out every meal. She takes me shopping and lets me get absolutely anything I want."

I opened my arms. "Absolutely anything?" All that was in Mica's room was one bag of clothes marked dirty and one marked clean. It had taken a message to Santa to get her a new swimsuit. "Where's all the junk she buys you?"

"I give lots of it away!" The tears were dripping off her chin but it all seemed so bogus. It was like a performance. So I clapped.

That's when Cody changed sides. He vaulted over to her bunk and began patting her on the back. *"I* believe you, Mica. Ben is so lactose intolerant! Are we going to meet her? Will she come here?"

"Can't," she snuffed. "She's *way* too busy performing in holiday galas."

"Galas," I said. "Tell me another one." Mica was describing some kind of grand opening to Cody when I went up the companionway ladder and back into the rain.

I didn't go back inside the houseboat. Instead I sat in the rocker on the deck. Through the open windows I could hear Mom and Dad inside making Christmas breakfast. Dad was singing "Jingle Bells," but it felt fake.

About now back home, Clay was knocking on Justin's door, Leroy was taking his new scooter for a test run on Magnolia. I wished I was there, hanging with them, instead of sitting alone on the deck of a houseboat in the rain.

Maybe I had it all wrong. Maybe Christmas is about doing the same old stuff with the same old people.

I didn't know what this was, but it sure wasn't Christmas.

chapter eighteen

THE BATTLE SCAR

I was drinking some of Mom's hot chocolate when Mica trailed Cody into the boat. "Look what Mica gave us for Christmas!" he said. The thing he set on the table had eyes and a tail. It looked like an underinflated ball, with prickles.

"I collected it myself." Mica pushed her bangs back. "It's a porcupine fish. I found it dried up like that on the beach."

"Beautiful!" Mom said, not touching it. "By the way, I like your swimsuit and cover-up."

Mica hugged her. "Santa brought them," she said.

Cody put a foot on his new scooter, but couldn't make it go on the rug. "We can't try our stuff out," he complained. "There's too much gravel in the parking lot. There's no place to shoot hoops. Plus, it's drizzling."

"Come on, Cody, we'll fish from under the bridge," Mica said, turning Cody toward the door. Dad handed me the new rods and gave me a shove. I was out the door too, even though I wasn't invited.

As I followed Mica and my brother down the gravel road alongside the canal I tried to think of someplace to go besides where they were going. There wasn't anyplace else.

Cody kept looking back, shooting me eye signals. He wanted me to apologize. But apologize for what? The girl was definitely a liar. After a while, he stopped looking back and just talked to her.

It was barely sprinkling, but cold without the sun. Cody and I both wore jeans and sweatshirts. The print on Mica's flapping cover-up glowed in the dim light. She had so many goose bumps her skin looked like sandpaper. "Hey! You want my sweatshirt?" I called. At first she pretended to be surprised I was back there. Then she made a big deal out of taking the shirt—like the loan meant we were going steady or something.

"I just don't want you to catch a cold," I said. I kicked a rock as hard as I could because I couldn't kick her.

"Have you two ever fished before?" She pulled my sweatshirt down to her knees.

"Go easy!" I said. "Do you mind not stretching it?"

"Ben fishes," said Cody. "He fishes all the time. He's good."

"As good as he is at swimming?" She pushed the sleeves of my sweatshirt up and grabbed the handle of the bait bucket. Two dozen live shrimp from the tank at the store sloshed as she walked along. Her rod bounced against her shoulder.

Cody skipped to keep up with her. I fell back.

The road dead-ended at Snake Creek. They turned left and walked under the bridge. When I caught up, they were standing around, not talking. It was dark and damp under there, and kind of creepy. The incline that ran up from the water's edge to where the bridge met the ground was a field of tumbled boulders. A car passed overhead, and the bridge boomed.

There were no fishermen on the boulders casting out into the creek, but they had definitely been there. Beer cans, plastic bait tubs, six-pack rings, and tangled wads of line were everywhere. Up the hill of boulders there was even a cast-off white T-shirt. "Dirty, rotten *Homo sapiens,*" Mica said.

"What's that Latin for?" Cody asked.

"Us," she said. "People. The *sapiens* part means full of wisdom."

"You can turn Latin into English? For the animal names too?"

"Sure. They usually mean things like 'slime foot' or 'with a spiny skeleton.' Stuff like that."

"Homo sapiens." Cody puffed his chest out. "Full of wisdom."

"That's just because we're the ones who make up the names." She kicked a plastic tub. It bounced off a boulder with a loud clatter.

As the echo pinged around under the bridge, the thing I had thought was a T-shirt flapped and let out a booming, *skraaaaaak!* Cody screamed. Mica fell off the rock she'd been standing on. "What the heck was that?" She scrabbled back up.

"Bet it's a great white heron," I said, jumping from rock to rock. "Or a common egret." I wasn't taking any chances. But as I got close I saw the killer-sharp beak with the white scar. And on either side, the beady little eyes of Slip-In-Easy. To be sure I checked the legs. Yellow. "Make that a heron," I called. Then more quietly I said, "Hello, Slip."

"Slip!" panted Cody, catching up. "Slip's our pet," he explained as Mica ran into him.

"I knew Slip before you," she said, steadying herself. "I used to feed him for Aunt Emma."

"Aren't you a mess?" I told the bird. He had gotten himself tangled in one of the piles of discarded fishing line. Monofilament was wrapped around a wing and a leg, binding them together. When he tried to move the leg, it twisted the wing back. He couldn't fly, he couldn't walk. But he could still give the evil eye.

"Poor old Slip." Cody crouched on a boulder.

Mica squatted too and shook her head. "Stupid *Homo sapiens.*"

Cody stared at the hog-tied bird, then turned to Mica. "What'll we do?"

"Cut him loose, of course." She reached for the heron. Slip stabbed at her with his beak.

I stuffed my hands in my pockets. "I'd try something else if I were you." He held his head up, neck crinked, ready to strike again. Hogtied or not, Slip still had the Attitude.

"We're here to help you, you dumb bird," Mica said. "Listen, you guys, I'm going to sneak around from the back and hold his wings against his body. Ben, you grab his head."

"What do you mean, grab his head?"

She stepped nonchalantly from rock to rock until she was behind Slip. "You know, grab it."

The heron's head swayed like a cobra, one beady eye on me. "Grab it *how?*" I asked.

"You're thirteen and a whole half. Figure it out." She swept Slip up in her arms, pinning the free wing against his side with her elbow. "Now, Ben! Do it!"

When I lunged, Slip's neck was whipping around like a hose with the water running full blast. I never got a hand on him. Not even a finger. As soon as I felt the breeze from his swinging head, I turned my face away and sat back on my butt.

"Hurry up!" Mica said, eyes squeezed shut. She was having a hard time holding on as Slip swung his beak around.

"Turn the bird loose," I told her. "There's got to be a better way. Somebody's going to lose an eye. Probably me."

"I don't believe this," she taunted. "Brother Ben's scared of a bird."

"I like having two eyes." I wasn't about to try again, but I was too mad to be careful, so I got a couple of inches closer than I meant to. I saw a blur of motion, then felt a sharp pain. I fell back, scraping my left arm on a boulder, cracking my tailbone on another one. Something warm oozed down my cheek. I touched the place. My fingers came back bloody.

"Let go, Mica!" Cody yelled. "Ben's hurt!" But Mica would let me bleed to death before giving up.

I felt dazed. Drops of blood fell on my jeans. Cody squirmed his arms out of his sweatshirt sleeves. "Don't worry, Ben," he said, pulling the sweatshirt over his head. I figured he was going to give it to me to stop the bleeding. Instead he made a wild toss. The sweatshirt covered Slip's head. Cody squished the thick fabric around it and held on. "Okay, I got it."

Mica opened an eye. "Cody?"

"I got it," he repeated. "Everything's under control."

Mica opened her other eye. "Way to go, Cody! Now, we need to cut the lines. Do either of you guys have a knife?"

"Great time to start thinking about it," I mumbled. But I got up on my knees and dug my pocketknife out. I cut the lines, being real careful not to nick the bird or Mica or my brother with the blade. We all got blood on us anyway. Mine.

I had to keep shrugging my shoulder to wipe away the blood running down my face. "Okay," I said, when the last thread of line snapped. "Turn him loose."

"What if he attacks?" asked Cody.

"Jump back when you let go, okay?" Mica said. She quit pressing Slip's wings to his sides. "Now, Cody!"

My brother jerked the shirt off Slip's head, then hid his own face with it.

Slip teetered. For a second I thought he was going to fall right on top of Cody, beak first. I snatched my brother out of the way. But Slip caught his balance. He opened his wings a little, then closed them. "Maybe something's broke," I said.

"If it is, we'll have to catch him all over again and take him to a vet," Mica answered.

With only the top of his head poking through the hole, Cody quit wrestling his sweatshirt back on. He blinked at us. "Whaddya mean, catch him again?" I could tell he wasn't ready to be brave again so soon.

Skraaaaak! Slip's wings snapped open. He pushed off with his yellow feet and hopped-flew over the tumbled boulders down to the water. He jumped off the last of the rocks. Wings beating hard, he turned toward the channel that cut out to the Atlantic. With a parting *skraaak,* he was gone.

The three of us sat. I shucked my T-shirt and held it to my cheek to stop the bleeding. "You brothers were so great!" Mica slapped an arm around each of our necks.

I pressed on the cut. "Cody was."

"You too. You almost lost an eye! Good work!"

"Cody's the hero," I said, mussing his hair. "Where'd you get the idea to cover the head, bro?"

Cody beamed. "When all else fails, think!"

I thought that was something Dad only said when we were messing around with cars. "When did Dad tell you that?"

He looked mystified. "Dad didn't tell me. You did."

We never got a line wet on our first fishing trip with our new rods. My face wouldn't quit bleeding. They dragged me into the marina store, both of them babbling about how the three of us had tackled the murderous Slip-in-Easy and won.

Dad held my chin and turned my face to the light. "Hey, soldier, sit on this stool and let me patch you up."

Once he'd assured Mom that the blood made it look worse than it was, Mom walked the other two back to the houseboat for ice cream. "You were both so brave," she said, putting an arm around each of them. "But next time come get us, okay?"

I didn't want to give Dad the details, so I changed the subject. "How come you opened the store? It's Christmas."

"I had to fix a broken steering cable," Dad said, swabbing the cut with peroxide. "The guy was taking his Christmas present for a spin and broke down. He pounded the houseboat window. Everyone knows how to find Uncle Bert." He whistled between his teeth. "Looks like you'll have a scar when this heals up."

Just what I needed. Another pointless scar to go with the one from the Winthrop's nippy beagle. I felt like the kid in *The Red Badge of Courage* who got his wound running away from the battle.

Dad squeezed ointment into the cut. "You're awful quiet for a hero."

"I'm not a hero! Cody's the hero, Cody and Mica."

"You're the one who's bleeding."

"Listen, Dad, it was a stupid accident," I told him. "I wasn't about to grab Slip's head. He was trying to gouge my eye out."

Dad put the cap back on the ointment. He covered the gash with a row of Band-Aids. "Go." He squeezed my neck. "Get yourself a bowl of ice cream."

"I don't want any."

"You know, Ben. There's a fine line between being brave and being stupid. Nothing wrong with knowing the difference." He shoved me toward the door.

I didn't go for ice cream. Instead, I walked back to the bridge and sat on the rocks.

I felt like crap. A scar is okay, but only if you get it by being brave. Rocky DeGarza would say the same.

chapter nineteen

THE BOTTOM OF
THE FOOD CHAIN

It rained the next day too. I helped Dad with a four-handed repair job on *Joe's Paycheck*. Uncle Bert's awning kept our heads dry, but drips off the canvas ran down our backs. Under the gravel was a white clay Dad called marl. It was slick as ice. "Watch your step," he said, but both of us took a few slides. If we hadn't caught ourselves on the gunnels of *Joe's Paycheck,* we would've gone straight down.

Rain seemed wetter in the Keys. It seeped into everything. Each time Dad sent me inside for parts, Mom, Mica, and Cody would be playing Monopoly at the counter. Even when they landed on Community Chest, they didn't seem to be having much fun. "Smells like old socks in here," Cody said. The damp made everything musty.

When we went back to the houseboat for lunch, we discovered a leak over the window by the dinette. Dad stuffed a towel between the window and the frame. It wasn't long before the towel started dripping.

Up home, when it rains, we play board games on the Lewis's dining room table. You have to look through a window and across the porch to even see the falling rain. From their table it looks far away. If we get tired of games there's the mall, or the dollar movie, or Skate World.

Here there was nothing but water falling on water. After lunch we all went back to the store. Cody took a slide on the wet dock and almost did a header into the canal.

The afternoon dragged. We all got a little crazy. Cody ran out on the deck of the store, leaned over the railing, and yelled, "Stop, rain! We want to *do* something!" But it went on all day long. Mica left the store to cook supper for her father. By the time Dad locked up for the night, Mica was heating something on the camp stove under the blue tarp. Cody ran over to check it out. "Dinty Moore Stew," he reported as we stepped aboard the *Loveboat*.

We were eating supper to the drip of the towel stuffed into the window when someone pounded on the door.

"Come in, Mica," Mom called.

Mica slid onto the bench beside me. "What're you eating?"

"Zucchini and toad food," Cody said.

"He means tofu," Mom said. Toad food is what my brother and I call it. It's more accurate.

"I've never had tofu before." I thought she looked discouraged, even before she took her first bite.

"Is your father at home?" Dad asked.

"Oh, he's home." Mica chewed and swallowed a bite. "He's definitely home. And he's in one of his moods." She watched the towel drip, then asked, "You brothers want to try fishing the bridge again while there's still a little light? We don't want to waste the whole day."

"Sure," said Cody. We pushed our dishes back, abandoning three plates of toad food—something we'd never get away with at home.

"I'll be over there to check on you in a little while," Dad promised as we took off. "No heron-wrestling, Ben."

Dr. Delano was sitting on the picnic table under the tarp we'd nailed up, smoking a small cigar. Beside him on the table was a canvas backpack.

"Good evening, sir," I said. "How are you?"

"I hate rain. I hate kids. I hate rain and kids together."

Mica grabbed my arm to hurry me past. "When it rains he gets stuck inside, teaching arts and crafts."

"I hate arts and crafts," he said, unbuckling the pack.

"The brothers and I are going fishing," Mica said. "Okay?"

"Fine, fine." He lifted a large jar out of the pack, held it up, and looked at what was inside.

Cody stopped dead in his tracks. "What's in the jar?"

Dr. Delano was probably wondering what he had to do to get away from kids. Then he looked at Cody. Cody was mesmerized. "Do you really want to know?" Dr. Delano asked. Cody nodded hard. My brother's curiosity usually gets him in trouble, but Dr. Delano seemed to be a sucker for curiosity. "Come take a look. You tell me." And he handed my brother the jar.

Cody pressed his nose to it, but his breath fogged the glass. He pulled his face back, then wiped the jar against his chest. He looked again. "A starfish?"

"That's right, a starfish."

Not to be outdone, Mica put her own nose up to the jar. "It's a thorny sea star, *Echinaster sentus.* One of the most common shallow-water sea stars of Southern Florida."

"You aren't gonna eat him, are you?" Cody asked.

Dr. Delano threw his head back and laughed. "No. I'm going to put him in one of our tanks," he said, taking the jar back. He unscrewed the lid, then stopped. "What do you say, Cody? Would you like to do the honors?"

Cody looked over his own shoulder, then touched himself in the middle of the chest. "You mean, put him in the tank? Me?"

"If you think you can do it gently."

Taking the jar in both hands, Cody poured the water into the tank slowly. The starfish slid out with the last of the water and drifted to the bottom, its legs curled and stiff. When it landed, it just sat there, not uncurling or anything. "Are you sure it's alive?" Cody asked.

"Wait," said Dr. Delano. "Watch." And in a few seconds the purple star relaxed and began to move across the bottom, although the five arms didn't seem to be doing anything.

"How's he do that?" Cody asked.

Dr. Delano leaned toward my brother. "Tube feet," he whispered. *"Podia."*

"Podia?" Cody whispered back.

Mica's dad winked. "That's right. Let me tell you about *podia.*"

"No, Captain, not the *podia* lecture! You're off work, and we're going fishing. Mica gave her father a quick kiss on the cheek and grabbed the back of Cody's shirt. "Come on, brothers."

"I don't mind," said Dr. Delano as she hustled us away. "Really."

"No, no, no," Mica scolded. "You're releasing the line at *exactly* the wrong time."

Without seeing cast one from me, Mica had appointed herself Cody's teacher on the art of casting. She was sure she knew way more about it than I did. "Put your finger on the line," she said. "Lightly. Jeez, you don't have to squeeze it to death, Cody. Just kind of rest it, okay?"

With a flick of the wrist I cast my shrimp out into the middle of the channel. Between the bridge pilings the rain clouds were finally breaking up. The water was turning orange in the sunset.

"I don't know why I'm even bothering," Mica went on. "It's not like you're going to catch a fish with that thing on your hook."

"I don't want to hurt a shrimp," my brother whimpered.

"I already told you, it doesn't hurt them," said Mica, checking to be sure that the point of her own hook was still sticking out of the shrimp's back.

"Yes it does, you know it does," my brother wailed.

Cody hadn't gotten over Mica's demonstration of how to bait a hook, which she'd described each step of the way. "You pierce the carapace just behind the head, then you shove the hook through the guts and poke it out again back here." It hadn't helped any that the shrimp spread his stalked eyes when the hook went in.

Cody had grabbed the first thing he saw in the tackle box. "I'd rather use this."

Now Mica swished a finger through the fringy thing that dangled off Cody's line. "Know what this is called, Cody? It's a ballyhoo skirt.

Fishermen put them around a dead ballyhoo to attract sailfish and dolphin."

"What's a ballyhoo?"

"A fish shaped like a cigar, only it has a beak. You put the skirt on it."

"You play dress-up a with dead fish?" he asked, reeling in until the ballyhoo skirt poinged against the top eye on the rod.

"You are hopeless, Cody Floyd. Hope-less."

My new reel ticked as I cranked the line in. "Keep trying," I said over my shoulder. "You'll catch on."

I heard his bale tick over and the rod whip back. Then, *spoing.* The bale flipped again and the ballyhoo skirt stopped, dancing three feet from his rod tip. Before Mica could lay into him again I said, "Let me help you with that, bro," and leaned my rod against a piling.

Mica cast her line in a long, sailing loop. "Don't you know about the food chain, Cody?" Her bait landed near the bridge pilings on the far side of the creek. She reeled in slowly. "Big things eat middle-sized things, and middle-sized things eat little ones." She lifted her line out of the water, shrimp swinging. "With a name like 'shrimp,' which end of the food chain do you think this guy is on?"

"It's not his fault he's small," Cody said.

A car rumbled across the bridge. The sun was sinking. I could just make out the pale washed denim of Mica's shorts and the shiny handles of the fishing pliers that poked out of her back pocket. The pliers were for pulling hooks out of fishes' mouths. So far she hadn't gotten close enough to a fish to use them.

I had to catch something, I didn't care what, before Dad corralled us. But first I had to see my brother get off at least one good cast.

"Watch how she does it," I whispered to Cody as Mica got ready to cast again.

She paused, listening as something with a small motor shot over our heads. "Sounds like the Captain's scooter," she said. "Wonder where *he's* going."

"You watching?" I whispered as she cocked her arm to cast. "First she flips the bale so the line can unwind. But see, she puts a finger on the line so it doesn't unwind until she wants it to." Mica cast. "No big deal, right? Easy as pitching a ball. Go for it, Cody." I gave him an encouraging slap on the butt.

Tock. Cody flipped the bale. *Sploop.* The ballyhoo skirt dropped like a giant spider. "Forgot to put your finger against the line," I said. "Try again."

Suddenly, I heard a noise like the crack of a rifle. I whipped around. "What was that?" Rings were spreading on the water.

"Tarpon!" Mica yelled. "Biggie!" She leapt from rock to rock, reeling in as she ran. She was still moving when she made the next cast. It fell short of the bull's-eye of ripples.

I grabbed my rod. With a sidearm cast I set my shrimp right in the middle of the ripples—a great cast. Mica wasn't watching. At that moment, in a completely different spot, the tarpon rose up on its tail. "See it, Ben?" she yelled. "It's huge! Colossal!" The tarpon shook its head, like it was laughing at us. When it fell over on its side the spray shot up three feet and out six.

Our reels ticked like mad, both of us pulling in line as fast as we could. *Zzzzzzz,* Mica's line sailed out. *Zzzzzzz,* mine followed.

"Poor shrimps," Cody moaned. "The poor, poor shrimps. First they get dragged through the water, then they fly through the air."

Crack! A second tarpon jumped farther down the creek, just off the end of the dock at Pirate's Bay. Then a third fish broached. The band on the deck at the resort began playing "Shake, Rattle, and Roll." The tarpon danced on their tails.

"Mica!" I shouted. "We need to get out on the water."

"Come on, brothers, to the Zodiac!" And she took off running, rod in one hand, bait bucket in the other. Cody couldn't keep up, so the two of us fell behind.

"The poor shrimps," Cody repeated, watching the swinging bait bucket vanish into the dusk. "The poor, poor shrimps. Bet their stomachs hurt."

chapter twenty

A RIDE WITH MR. TROUBLE

By the time we got to the dock Mica was in the Zodiac, engine running, bait bucket between her feet. Dad held the bowline. "But Mr. Floyd," she begged. "You *have* to let us go. You don't understand! There are tarpon out there!"

I knew Dad didn't like the idea of us out on the water after dark—but he *did* understand about tarpon. That meant we could go, but only after he had handed out PFDs, checked our running lights, given us an extra flashlight, and told us to stick close to the mouth of the canal. Twice. "That means this side of the bridge," he added.

"We will," I said, itching to go. We heard another splash from out on Snake Creek. Me and Cody climbed aboard. "Hit it!" I urged, and Mica revved the motor up.

We had just reached the end of the canal when the music at Pirate's Bay stopped. "Me and the boys are getting a tad-bit dry," said the voice over the loud speaker. "We're going to take us a little break now, but don't go away. Big Ed and the Fishin' Fools will be back in twenty minutes."

Then Big Ed turned off his mike. The Evinrude sounded awful loud all of a sudden. When we hit the middle of the creek, Mica throttled back and put it in neutral. She reached for her rod. *Zzzzzzz,* her line sang. Her shrimp landed with a splash.

Zzzzzzz, I cast the other way, upcreek.

We cast and reeled in, cast and reeled in. "Where are they?" I asked.

As if it had heard me, a tarpon jumped. We both cast to the splash, but we were just out of range.

It happened over and over. We'd reel in and motor a couple hundred feet, then try again. Nine times out of ten, the next jump would come from the piece of water we'd just left. Cast, reel in, move. We chased the elusive splash up and down the creek.

Then for a while nothing jumped at all. I worked with Cody. He got off a couple of semi-okay casts—his ballyhoo skirt flew a few feet before landing.

Mica caught a small catfish. "Keeper?" I asked. Me and Dad catch cats in Lake Talquin sometimes.

"They taste like old sneakers," she said. Using the pliers, she held the hook by its shank and jiggled until the fish dropped back in the water.

I caught a grunt. "Keeper?" I asked as it opened its mouth and grunted at me.

"Only if you think you can catch about a dozen more," Mica said.

Fish number two went back in the creek.

Big Ed and the Fishin' Fools finished easing their thirst and launched into a song that seemed to be called "Cheeseburger in Paradise." Tarpon rose on their tails. Mica and I went back to chase and cast, chase and cast. Cody kept casting his ballyhoo skirt. He didn't aim for the tarpon rings, he just liked dragging the lure through the water. "It pulls like a fish," he said as he reeled it in.

"Hey, Ben. Top this." Mica sailed a shrimp toward the bank, landing it between the roots of two mangroves. "Perfect cast."

Being careful not to cross my line over hers, I landed my cast so close our two shrimp could shake hands.

"Come on, Cody," she urged. "Three for three."

Cody cast, but the ballyhoo skirt popped straight up, then plummeted. *Splash.*

"Oooooh," Mica said, looking over the side. "Nice one."

My brother laid his rod down. "I'm no good at this," he said. His lure still hung in the water, flapping in the current.

He was scratching his arm when the fish lifted its immense head out of the water and sucked down his hook, ballyhoo skirt and all.

"Tarpon!" Mica yelled.

Cody let out a surprised yelp and snatched the rod as it went over the side.

Zing! His fishing line snapped taut. *Zwang!* The raft spun. The bow had been pointing toward the bridge, but the tarpon turned us one-eighty and towed the Zodiac down the creek. Water poured over the bow. "Flip the bale, Cody! Flip the bale!" I knew the instant he did it, because the bow popped up and there we sat, dead in the water.

"Did I lose him?" Cody asked.

Line was stripping off his reel like mad, free-spooling as the fish surged away from us. "No," I said. "He's still on." I reached across, flipped the bale back on, and held my breath. Chances were the line would break as soon as that tarpon stretched it tight.

The Zodiac had a self-bailing feature, but Mica was dipping water out with her hands when Cody's line lifted out of the water, tight and straight, and the Zodiac began to move again. It went slow at first, with the water we'd taken on sloshing under the seats. But we went faster and faster as the big fish picked up speed. We were headed down the creek at an angle that brought us steadily closer to shore.

I pulled an oar out of its holder to keep us away from the tangled roots of the mangroves. While I fought off mangroves, Pirate's Bay became a smudge of light behind us. The band faded until it was like the background music in a movie.

"Dad told us to stick around the canal," said Cody, holding on for dear life.

"We aren't the ones leaving the canal!" I panted. Heart pounding in my ears, I thought, I wouldn't trade this for back home, not in a million years. "Tighten the drag a little, would ya, Cody?"

"Don't do it," Mica snapped. "He's not tired enough yet. Wear him out a little first."

"Okay, Cody," I said. "Let 'er run."

As we water-skied behind the tarpon Cody yelled, "Hah! You're not gonna get away from me, Mr. Trouble."

Any time the line went slack Mica and I shouted, "Reel in, reel in!" We didn't want to give Mr. Trouble enough line to tie knots around the snags at the edge of the creek. "Reel!" we'd shout, and Cody would reel like crazy.

Each time he felt Cody pulling back, the tarpon leapt and shook his huge head. Water sprayed off his silver scales. "Give him a little slack," Mica shouted. "Bow to the king when he jumps. Don't let him throw the hook!"

Then the fish dove, the reel screamed, and the tug of war went on.

"Coming about!" yelled Mica as the turning Zodiac bucked up on one edge.

"The line cut my finger, Ben!"

I didn't have time to look at Cody's finger. "Butts down!" I yelled. "Park it, or swim with Mr. Trouble." Me and Cody dropped off the seat; Mica slid from the pontoon down to the stiff rubber floor. We soaked our butts good.

"Ben! I gotta let go," Cody wailed. "My arms are gonna pop!"

"Mica, take this!" I shoved the oar back toward her, reached over Cody, and lifted the rod out of his hands. I felt the pull of that big fish all the way to the roots of my hair. "Wow, Cody. How'd you hang on for so long?"

"I'm stronger than you think," he said.

I glanced up and yelled. "Hey! He's charging the bridge!" We were headed straight for it. The bridge grew fast, like in some action-adventure movie. My arm muscles screamed. It just doesn't get any better than this, I thought.

"Oh, look," Mica said, ignoring the bridge. "There's the Captain." As we zoomed by she waved to her father, who was at the bar. "I hope he's not drinking too much."

I shouted, "Mica!" We were headed straight for the first bridge piling.

"What?" she said. "It's just the bridge." She braced the oar against the piling and shoved. The tarpon hauled us over to the next piling and tried again.

"I'm getting tired of this." Mica stood, and pushed off with both arms.

The Zodiac yawed. Mica wheeled her arms like she was about to flip over the side. Holding the rod with one hand, I reached up and grabbed the front of her shorts. "Park it," I said. She still fell, but at least she did it inside the boat.

"Uh-oh," said Cody. "See where we are?" Mr. Trouble had towed us out from under the bridge and into the channel.

The tide was dead low, the channel a ribbon of moonlight between sand flats. Ahead, the black silhouettes of the channel markers pointed the way to the deep, unmarked waters of the Atlantic.

"Ben?" said my brother. "What're we gonna do?"

"Would you let me think a minute?" I said. The quickest thing would be to cut the line. I didn't want to cut the line.

"Mission Control," Mica said. "We have a problem." When I looked up I realized she wasn't talking about being towed out to sea, which was a slow-moving kind of disaster. A cruiser that had been speeding toward the marker at the entrance to the channel had just made the turn. It bore down on us, barely slowing.

"Hey, hey!" Cody and Mica shouted and waved their arms. I shouted too, but I hung onto the rod. Mica stood and raised the paddle. "Stop! Don't run us down!"

Then, all we could see was the white eye of the cruiser's bow light, big and blinding. Cody screamed. The pitch of the engine dropped. The pilot had pulled back on the throttle. A voice called, "You kids all right?"

"Yeah, we're fine," I said, trying to feel the tug of that giant fish. Where are you, Mr. Trouble, you still there?

"We're *not* fine," Cody whined. "We went under the bridge. You heard Dad." But as the boat passed us, the Zodiac began to turn. The giant tarpon had reversed course again and was towing us slowly back under the bridge. My arms felt like bags of wet cement, but I didn't care. My fish was still on the line.

"Ben?" Dad stood at the end of the dock. "I told you to stick around the canal. You bring it back in here right now, bud!"

Mica yelled. "Cody hooked a giant tarpon, Mr. Floyd!"

"A giant tarpon? Really?" Dad the authority figure and Dad the fisherman were fighting for control. "Way to go, Cody!" Dad the fisherman raised an arm as we went slowly by.

Cody reached. "Give me the rod, Ben. I'm not tired any more."

"You sure? He's still fighting pretty hard." He wasn't, but I wanted to reel that tarpon in awful bad.

Cody tried to take the rod. I held on. "Give it, Ben! He's *my* fish."

"I fought him way longer than you. And it wasn't like you caught him with skill or anything. You got lucky." I imagined the story I'd tell when I got home—a fight to the death between me and Mr. Trouble.

"But it's my rod!" He punched me in the back. "Santa brought it!"

"Okay, okay. Quit whining." I shoved the rod into his hand.

He cranked the handle. Little by little, the line came out of the water. I didn't notice that the fish had towed us into the boat basin at Pirate's Bay until I saw the drops hanging on the line turn red and green, catching the colors of the Christmas lights on the dock.

About ten feet from the boat, a rolling flash of silver twisted up through the dark water. It broke the surface, then disappeared.

Cody stopped reeling. "There's something I want to tell you guys," he said. "This is my fish, right?"

"It sure is," said Mica.

"Ben?"

"Yeah, it's yours, Cody."

"Here's the thing," he said. "We're not gonna eat my fish. We're gonna let him go."

Mica laughed as she paddled toward the dock by the motel—the tarpon was so tired we were dragging him. "Nobody eats tarpon, Cody. They're just fun to catch."

When we got near the dock, Mica climbed over the side. The water was up to her waist. "Bring him over here," she said. Cody stood. Swinging the rod, he walked the fish around to her side.

We looked down. The tarpon was as long as Cody's fishing rod, each scale as big as a silver dollar. All the fight had gone out of him; he seemed half-dead. "I'll need help," Mica said. "Get in the water, Ben."

"You poor old fish." Cody leaned over the side. "I'm sorry. I didn't mean to catch you."

I slid into the cool water. The fish was huge, but I wasn't scared. I respected him. Just maybe, if he knew I was the one who fought him so hard, he respected me too.

Mica pulled the pliers out of her back pocket. There was a click as she locked them on the shank of the hook.

"Well, would ya look at that!" Big Ed's voice boomed out of an amplifier. "Those kids have got themselves one decent tarpon. Let's give them a big round of applause." Suddenly, the crowd on the deck turned our way. Some of them started whooping and stamping. I looked for Mica's dad but didn't see him. Maybe he'd gone home while we were fighting the tarpon.

Mica used both hands to lift the fish up on the pliers. In a moment the weight of the tarpon pulled the hook out, along with the plastic hula skirt lure.

"Swim," Cody whispered. "Go on, you're free."

But the fish just lay in the water. "Come on, Ben," Mica said. "You get on one side of him, I'll get on the other."

A couple of men wandered over from the deck, beer cans in their hands. "Bet that sucker weighs a hundred pounds," said one.

"Bet you five bucks it's closer to one-fifty," said the other.

"Easy enough to find out." The first one grabbed the big metal hook of the dock scale with one hand and twisted it back and forth.

"No!" Cody shouted. "He's my fish! We're gonna turn him loose, not hang him up by his lips." He leaned over and put a hand on his fish's side.

"Don't pay them any attention," said a guy in a white shirt and pants. "They're just a couple of drunks. Let me help you revive him." He kicked off his flip-flops.

"That's okay. We know what we're doing," Mica said. "Slide your hands under him," she whispered. Together we walked Mr. Trouble around in the shallow water.

"What're you doing?" Cody asked.

"Artificial respiration for fish," said the man, sliding his sandals back on. "They're moving the water over his gills."

"Come on, Trouble," I urged, feeling no motion from the cool, heavy fish in my arms. He couldn't be dead. Just couldn't. "Come on, swim."

As we pulled him through the water, the fish began to feel different. Kind of like a bike tire getting up to pressure. Suddenly, something slammed me in the ribs. It felt like I'd been hit with a baseball bat. As the fish streaked away, I tried to catch my breath. I saw one last silver flash—then he was gone.

Cody cheered. Pretty soon everyone was cheering—even the guys with the five-dollar bet.

"Mica, is that you?" Dr. Delano had come out of the inside bar. "What are you doing here?" He sounded baffled.

"Keep up!" Big Ed yelled into the mike. "That little girl caught herself a big old tarpon."

"Did you release it?" Mica's father asked.

"Of course we did," said Mica, hoisting herself out of the water.

"Good, good." He looked a little unsteady on his feet. "You take care of Mother Ocean, she takes care of you."

Mica put a wet arm around her father's waist. "Time to go home, Captain." He leaned on her heavily as she led him over to the scooter. "You think you brothers can take the Zodiac across the creek?" she called.

"No problem," I shouted back.

Dr. Delano lifted his bad leg over the bike. Mica slid in front of him and kicked the starter. The scooter wobbled, then picked up speed.

I started the Evinrude and headed out into the creek. It was just a short trip to the other side, but it felt good to be at the helm.

Cody pushed the perforated door of the bait bucket and shined a flashlight inside. "Three left." He dumped the bucket over the side. The shrimp swam away making little V-shaped trails in the moonlit water. "Good luck, guys," he said.

When we reached the canal, Dad trotted up the dock alongside us, flashlight in hand. "Did you land it?"

"We didn't get it on land," Cody said. "We let him go."

We were pulling into the spot behind the *Martina* when the beam of Dad's flashlight hit my shirt. Something sparkly was stuck to the front of it. A giant scale from a giant tarpon. I put it in my pocket. Some souvenir.

chapter twenty-one

CHICKEN FIGHTERS

We had been lazing around in the canal for hours when Dad came down the dock. "How's the water?" he asked. "That's for us to know and for you to find out," Mica answered. Then she did an underwater handstand.

He took his wallet out of his pocket and set it on a piling.

"Dad...you need your swimsuit," said Cody.

Dad's leather belt flapped as he yanked it through the loops.

"You really do, Dad," I said as he hung the belt over a piling. But it looked like me and Cody were in for a major embarrassment.

Off came the T-shirt. Dad's hairy gorilla chest was on display. His right moccasin hit the deck. Standing on one foot, he grabbed the toe of his sock and pulled.

"About that swimsuit, Dad...," I said as the sock sproinged off.

The sock landed. "You boys think I need a suit?" His left shoe hit the dock.

"Afraid so," I said.

He grabbed the toe of his other sock and pulled. "Then maybe I'll go put one on." The second sock landed. "Should I? Nah." Down to his greasy work cutoffs, he jumped.

I bet his wake slapped the other shore of the Atlantic. He came up spouting like a whale. "Who wants to dive off my shoulders?"

"Me," said Mica, who was already swimming over to him.

"No, me," said Cody.

"Sorry, son. Ladies first." And Dad held out a hand.

For a while they took turns climbing up on his shoulders and diving. Mica showed off her back flips. Cody showed off his belly flops.

At five, Mom locked up the store. As soon as she saw us, she took off her watch and put it with Dad's belt. "Mom," Cody called. "You need a—"

Her skirt spread like a flower in the air, then, *splash,* she was in the water too. She pushed her streaming hair back from her face. "Nice," she said.

Of course she had to dive off Dad's shoulders too, which was kind of hard with her wet skirt stuck to her legs. "I have an idea," she said when she came up from her dive. "Chicken fights."

"Chicken fights! Yes!" shouted Cody.

Mica circled Mom. "What's a chicken fight, Mrs. Floyd?"

"A chicken fight is one of the romantic things Mr. Floyd and I used to do when we were dating. Right, Mike?"

"One of the many," Dad said. "We'd pile the whole gang in my old Ford Falcon and head for Cape San Blas or St. George Island."

"Remember those guys? Mick and Lindy, Squeak and the Toad," Mom recited.

"And Rita," Cody added. "You forgot Rita."

"That's right," said Mom, shaking a finger at Dad. "You kind of liked Rita." Mom would be a hundred and she would still be accusing Dad of kind of liking Rita.

"Did not, I swear! Her eyes were like this." Dad crossed his eyes.

"Mom, Dad," said Cody. "Could you please get to the part about chicken fighting?"

Dad uncrossed his eyes. "Are you saying we're off task?" Sometimes Dad sounds way too much like a teacher. "Oh yes, we were talking about chicken fighting. Well, the best way to describe a chicken fight is to have one." And Dad dove.

"Whoa... Dad, Dad!"

Cody rose out of the water, clinging to Dad's ponytail. My father flapped his folded arms and crowed. "Chicken number one, reporting for duty."

Mom grinned. "Want to be my partner, Mica?"

"Sure!" In a moment Mica was perched on Mom's shoulders.

"Chicken fighters, here are the rules," Dad said. "No scratching, no biting, no eye gouging. No elbows, no teeth. Just knock each other in the water, fair and square. Got it? Big Ben takes on the winner."

"Got it!" Cody shouted, reaching for Mica. He lasted half a second. She lunged, grabbed him around the waist, and twisted. Cody's legs kicked the air, then he plunged, making a huge splash.

Mica's arms shot up over her head. "Yes!"

Cody came up spluttering. "You're supposed to wrestle."

"I thought I was supposed to knock you in the water."

"Not right away! Not first thing!"

Mica hung down and looked into Mom's eyes. "Is that right?"

Mom looked up. "It *is* more fun if it lasts a while."

"Okay, got it." Mica hooked her feet behind Mom's back and waited for chicken number one to pull itself together. Technically, it was my turn, but Floyds are big on second chances.

Dad charged, and Mica latched onto Cody's wrists. He struggled until his face turned red. Then, suddenly, she let go and lunged. She locked her arms around his chest, then lifted and dropped him in one quick move. The girl was good.

"No fair!" Cody bellowed as soon as he'd popped back up. "You were going to make it last that time!"

"Ben?" said Dad. "You want to give it a try?"

Not really. If I lost I'd be a wimp. If I won I'd be a bully. Besides, there was something weird about hugging Mica, which was what chicken fighting came down to. That's what made it so romantic. "No thanks. I'll pass."

Mica rested her elbows on top of Mom's head. "Afraid you'll lose?"

"Go on, Ben, show her. Do it," Cody pestered. "Knock her little butt in the water!"

"Think you can knock my butt in the water?" she taunted. "I'd like to see you try."

I sighed and climbed on Dad's shoulders. As the cool air hit my wet chest I looked back at Cody. He stood in shallow water near the dock, eyes glued to me, Big Ben, little-brother avenger. He gave me the thumbs-up. I had my instructions: knock her little butt in the water, *now.*

Mica locked her feet behind Mom's back. Her hands became claws. We swayed like camel riders as Dad and Mom slogged toward each other. I let out a yelp of surprise when Mica dug her nails into my arms. I'd assumed the rules applied to her too.

I grabbed her around the ribs. We seesawed back and forth. She couldn't fall because she had her hooks in me. "No nails," I said between my teeth, but she didn't let go. What was wrong with her? Why did she want to win so bad?

"Go Ben! Go Ben!" My cheerleader by the dock was jumping up and down. "What are you waiting for?" What *was* I waiting for? I was getting tired of having her claws in my arm, so I tried something different. She was all braced to keep me from knocking her off backwards, so I just jerked her forward. And she went down.

"Chicken in the soup!" Cody yelled.

I raised my arms thinking, man that was *so* easy. Then Mica came up...crying!

"What's the matter, honey?" Mom thrashed over to her and dragged her into the shallows. She hugged the girl against her wet blouse. "Did he hurt you?"

"Hurt her?" There I sat, gaping holes in both arms from her talons. "All I did was put her little butt in the water—and without breaking any rules, I might add."

The crying got louder, then turned jerky like something rough was caught in her throat. Mom smoothed a hand down her back.

"I didn't do a thing, Dad," I said softly.

"I don't think this is about chicken fighting," Dad answered.

Mica hung on my mother. Mom was rocking her back and forth. "Just let it out, sweetie, let it out."

Forgetting it was his idea to knock her butt in the water, Cody hugged Mica too. "Why are you crying? Did water go up your nose?"

"I hit my head on the way down," she sobbed.

"On what?" I asked Dad. "There's nothing but water on the way down." Disgusted, I slid off his shoulders, then swam away underwater. When I came up, Mica was laughing; Cody and Mom were laughing. They fell against each other, helpless as a litter of puppies. I paddled back over to Dad, the only sane one in the bunch. "What happened to the waterworks? What's going on?"

"Group therapy," Dad said.

In the background I heard the scooter and saw Dr. Delano cut into the parking lot. He climbed stiffly off the bike and walked it along the dock. Head down, he leaned on the bike as if he needed it to keep him from falling over.

"Care to join us in the pool, Doctor?" Dad shouted.

Dr. Delano blinked as if he was just waking up.

"We're chicken fighting!" Mica pranced in the shallow water. "We can be a team."

He rubbed his eyes with one hand. "A chicken-fighting team." His voice was flat.

"Please," Mica begged. "It'll be fun."

"A chicken-fighting team," he repeated.

He put a hand on the piling, lifted a foot, and slowly unlaced his boot. He glanced at the shriveled socks Dad had flung on the dock, but tucked each of his own inside the proper boot. He took his wallet out of his pocket and set it beside Dad's.

Mica was going wild. Her father was going to team up with her!

He unbuttoned his shirt and shrugged out of it. His chest was as bald as mine.

When his belt hung like a second snake beside my father's, he lifted the pith helmet and carefully set it on top of everything else.

He emptied the pockets of his shorts into the helmet, then he let out a yip and pulled up his knees. *Spa-lash!*

Mom looked a little embarrassed as she hauled herself out to start supper, wet clothes clinging. Mica and Cody carried on the chicken fighting tradition without me. I'd had all I could take of being punctured and Mica-hugged.

I got my mask and snorkel. As I kicked around with my mask in the water I could hear the others laughing. Even Dr. Delano.

chapter twenty-two

THE HUMAN LIGHTBULB

We'd fished on the Bay all day, the sun beating down on us. Supper over, it should've been peaceful floating on our backs in the canal looking up at the stars—but Cody wouldn't quit pestering. "Let me take 'em off for a teeny eeny minute," he begged. "You know I can swim. Please…"

"It's not up to me," I said for the twenty-seventh time. "Mom won't let you night-swim without them." And I won't let you swim without them, period, I added to myself. A week and a half wasn't enough time to learn to swim—even for a kid who thought he already knew how.

"Water-wing baby!" Mica taunted.

"Ben, make Mica quit calling me a water-wing baby!"

"Mica, quit being a pain."

Mica was quiet a second, then she grabbed Cody by a wing and turned him. "Look over there, Cody, above the Coast Guard station. That's Orion."

"Where?" Cody asked.

"Right up there. See those three bright stars? That's his belt. The two up there are his shoulders; the other two sort of bright ones are his knees." She picked the stars out for him, the way Mom had done when she showed us the constellation.

"I know, I know," Cody sputtered. "I see the stars. I don't see the guy."

Shoosh... From above we heard the *Martina's* hatch slide. Dr. Delano climbed up on deck and stood in the square of light that came through the hatch. He held his pith helmet in both hands. "Mate?"

"Down here, Captain."

"I thought I'd go across the creek and listen to the band a while." He turned the pith helmet, sliding his fingers along the brim. "You'll be okay, don't you think? You have the brothers for company."

She paddled toward the *Martina* and hung on a rope. "Stay home tonight, please?"

"I won't be gone long." He climbed off the sailboat and unlocked the scooter.

"Be careful, Captain."

Her father lifted a finger to show he'd heard. He took off from the parking lot with a splat of gravel. The scooter crossed the drawbridge, a small light traveling fast. "Slow down, Captain," she whispered.

I lay back and fanned my arms. Across the creek the notes of the bass guitar pulsed, the lead guitar twanged. The water felt soft and warm. I locked my hands behind my head and floated. Cass would like this, I thought, floating, attached to nothing. Bet this is how she feels when she runs.

I thought again about getting in a car and taking off. And this time I put Cass in the passenger seat. I was a long way from the guys—too far for them to see inside my head.

"And that's the Big Dipper," Mica said. I followed the line of her shiny, wet arm. "Now, go out from the two stars at the front of the dipper." Her finger traced a line across the sky. "The first bright star you come to is the North Star. That's the star sailors steer by. It doesn't change positions with the seasons. The Captain and I use it when we're running at night."

Running at night. The words caught and carried me. I imagined I was the one aboard the *Martina*, skimming over dark water, chasing stars. But what I was imagining was Mica's *real* life, action packed, full of danger.

I rolled over and looked at the houseboat. Its ropes were crusted with sea life from hanging in the water. Technically it could go places—but it never did. Compared to the *Martina*, it was as mobile as a trailer set on concrete blocks.

Seeing Dad through the houseboat window, I felt disloyal. It wasn't that I wasn't having a great time. I was. The things I was doing here beat home by a mile. Fishing in the bay, I'd caught my first snook. Cody felt so sorry for it I had to throw it back. Still, I'd caught it. And then we went through a cut called Toilet Seat Channel. The markers were toilet seats nailed to poles. When was the last time I'd seen anything like that up home?

But even here, my life was Disney World compared to Mica's. No real adventure. And if anything remotely dangerous came along—like freeing Slip—I worried about losing an eye or something dumb like that and missed out.

"I have an idea,' Cody said. "Let's have a splashing contest!" He started to kick. She joined right in.

I moved a few strokes away. Splashing around with Mica might be exciting to Cody, but I wanted more. Adventure, speed, wheels. And there were other things too—things under the words that didn't seem to have names. I only knew that they were missing.

A silver thread of light streaked across the black sky. The splashing stopped. "Meteorite!" yelled Cody.

"Nuh-uh," Mica said.

"Yes-huh."

"For your information," she said. "It's a meteor when it's in the sky. It's only a meteorite after it lands."

The meteor disappeared. It had probably sizzled down in the sea somewhere. "So, *now* it's a meteorite," I said.

"That's what I was talking about," Cody told her. "I meant after it landed."

"No you didn't, you meant—"

"Hey." Cody lifted his head. "Do you guys smell popcorn?"

Mica poked her head up and sniffed too. "Popcorn with butter."

Just then, Mom stepped out on the deck of the *Loveboat,* a bowl of popcorn on her hip. "Race ya!" Cody whooped. And he kicked hard for the dock.

Mica dove under him. She swam like a dark fish beneath the water. Cody's salty spray stung my cheek where Slip had nailed me, so I pulled ahead of him. I was doing a sloppy dog paddle, when I let out a yell and jammed my feet into the mud.

I stood up, expecting to see a knife sticking out, but my chest was still wet, shiny, and hairless. The same old chest. Why did it hurt so bad? "Mom?" I croaked, gulping air and music and stars.

Mom was kneeling on the dock next to Mica. "What is it, honey?" The popcorn was scattered. "What's the matter?"

"Something stung me," Mica gasped. "Man-of-war maybe." She held one arm cradled in the other as if it was in a sling.

I crawled up on the dock, my breath whooping in and out like I'd just run a mile. Mom turned. "No! Not you too, Ben."

"Where's Cody?" I looked around for my brother, but I couldn't see him. "Cody!" I hollered.

I heard a commotion under the dock and Cody crawled out. "What's up, you guys? What happened? Aw, Mom, you spilled the popcorn."

We stood in a row on Aunt Emma's rug, dripping. "Cody's fine," Dad said after checking my brother out. "Ben?" The mark on my chest, which stung like the devil, looked like a skinny rope burn about two inches long. Pretty unimpressive. Dad looked at it for half a second. "Ben'll live."

Then he came to Mica. "Whoa!" As usual, she had done things bigger and better. A huge welt wrapped her upper arm. Another one crossed her thigh. Her face was the worst. The angry red mark went across one eyelid, then down her cheek and neck. Whatever had flicked my chest had clobbered her.

Dad had Mica hold her arm under the tap in the sink. He lifted a thin piece of tentacle off with the blade of a table knife.

Mica waited, water dribbling off her elbow, while Dad made a paste of meat tenderizer and water. "Aunt Emma's cure," he said, stirring it. Mom slathered Mica. She put a dab on my chest.

Still holding her arm up, Mica began to pace. She couldn't seem to stand still. "Portuguese man-of-war, Latin name, *Physalia physalis, Physalia physalis.*" Suddenly, she sat. "My lips are tingling." She rocked in her seat. "I feel all jangly and electric. I bet I would glow in the dark."

"Mica, the human lightbulb!" Cody chimed in. No one laughed. Mica jumped up and paced again.

"Aunt Emma's cure isn't enough," Mom told Dad in a low voice. "We need to get these kids to the emergency room."

"I'm okay," I said. "But you better take Mica." I wasn't *that* okay. My chest felt like it was on fire, but compared to Mica's, my injury was as serious as a stubbed toe. No one goes to the ER for a stubbed toe.

"We need her father's permission," Dad said. A teacher, he didn't take a kid anywhere without a signed permission slip. "Is your father aboard the *Martina?*"

"Across the creek," Mica gasped. "Listening to music." As she rocked, tears slid out from under her closed eyelids and dribbled off her chin. "My heart is going too, too fast."

"I'm taking her," Mom said. "Now."

Dad nodded. "I'll go across the creek and tell her father."

Mom turned to me. "Are you sure you don't want to come too, Ben?"

Ignoring the knife sticking me in the ribs I said, "Hey, I'm fine, Mom."

"Then run over to the sailboat and get clothes for Mica."

Normally, I wouldn't be caught dead picking through a girl's clothes, but this was an emergency. Digging in the bag marked

"Clean," I pulled out one T-shirt after another; it seemed like that was all there was in the bag. I threw one on the bunk, then pawed through the bag again, looking for clean shorts. There weren't any. I picked up the scrunched pair on the floor with my toes and flipped it onto the bunk.

That brought me to the part I didn't want to think about—underwear. I didn't even look for a bra. She had nothing to put in one. But she had to wear panties. I guess most girls had lots, but Mica lived in a swimsuit. I dug through the bag again, then dumped it on the berth. Finally, I found one little shriveled pair with teddy bears printed all over it. I picked it up by the elastic, dropped it on the shorts and shirt and rolled everything together. I snatched the turquoise flip-flops off the floor. Hugging the bundle, I ran up the companionway ladder.

"Mariner's Hospital is just past the Winn Dixie," Dad said. "You'll see the signs."

"You sure you aren't coming, Ben?" Mom asked. I shook my head, no. My sting burned like heck. I even had some of that lip-tingling Mica had mentioned. But when I lifted my shirt for the doctor, he'd laugh. All he'd see would be a little pink line. Cody rode along with Mom and Mica. I stayed put.

"Come on," Dad said as soon as we heard Aunt Emma's pickup pull away. "It's time for the Floyd men to get a marine biologist off his bar stool."

With Dad in the stern, the Zodiac sat low in the water. I untied the lines; he started the Evinrude. We motored down the canal in silence. A powerboat was anchored in the creek just off the bridge, lights trained on the water. Two kids holding long-handled nets stood on the transom. "What're they doing, Dad?"

"Shrimping." Normally, he would have given me the full shrimping lecture; tonight he was Dad-on-a-mission.

We motored into the boat basin as the band started playing the

"Cheeseburger in Paradise" song. There was one funny line about vegetarian food I wanted to remember so I could tell Mom. Mica's dad probably knew the words by heart. He heard it every night.

Dad tied the Zodiac to a piling and we climbed out at the spot where Mica and I had revived the tarpon. My father looked at the metal hook of the scale like he was thinking of hanging Mica's dad up on it.

But we didn't see Dr. Delano. We walked around the picnic tables, dodging dancers. "Sorry," Dad said, steadying the tray of beers he had almost knocked out of a woman's hand.

I spotted him first. He was sitting on the last stool at the outdoor bar. This is bad, I thought. I didn't know what a colleague was supposed to look like, but I didn't think the woman next to him in the black dress with half her boobs showing fit the description. Justin once said his mom thought his dad messed around, which was hard to believe since Mr. Riggs is about as good-looking as a hard-boiled egg. But Dr. Delano looks okay—not that I'm an expert on guys. Anyway, the woman in the plunging dress was acting like he was okay. She put her hand on his back and leaned toward him to say something in his ear.

I grabbed Dad's arm. "Over there." I said it quick so we could get this over with before Dr. Delano did something, like hold her hand—or worse.

I felt my father stiffen. The wrath of Dad was about to fall.

He moved through the crowd, shouldering people aside. He stopped barely two feet from Mica's father's stool. "Dr. Delano."

Mica's father had been laughing at something the lady had said. He was still smiling when he turned toward us. He must have seen how angry my father was because his voice kind of squeaked. "Mr. Floyd? Can I buy you a drink?"

Dad crossed his arms. "My wife has taken Mica to the emergency room at Mariner's."

Jeez, Dad, I thought. Couldn't you ease into it a little?

But Dad was in no mood to ease in. He wanted his words to have an effect.

And did they ever. Dr. Delano jumped to his feet. "What's wrong with my daughter?"

"She swam into a man-of-war. Got stung pretty bad."

"Who's going to pay for the drinks?" asked the colleague in the black dress, but Dr. Delano was already halfway to the scooter.

Hey!" Dad chased him. "We don't need two accidents. Are you sober enough to drive this thing?"

"Of course," Dr. Delano said, and he roared out of Last Pirate.

"They gave her a shot," Cody told me when they got back. "A big one. In the butt."

Mom put Mica to bed on our couch. Cody fell right to sleep in his berth. I slept too, but woke up lots of times. Each time I did I heard the adults' voices. They sat on the porch for hours, talking.

Once I heard Mica's dad say, "It would be so much easier if there were a woman to help me look after her. She needs a female role model." As I drifted back to sleep, I thought of the colleague in the black dress. Now *there* was a role model.

Sometimes it was Mica's voice that woke me up, or the sound of her pacing. Once, when I stuck my head out of our room, she was lying on the couch, holding onto the fringe at the edge of Mom's shawl. Mom was humming softly.

Dr. Delano stood a few feet away. When Mica let out a groan he covered his face with a hand.

"You'll be all right," Mom said, smoothing the hair back off Mica's forehead. "Hush, you'll be fine."

chapter twenty-three

KEY WEIRD

They're going to kill me today," Dr. Delano predicted. He was about to take off for a day of fun camp on zero sleep. Mom armed him with a handful of vitamins. He slugged them down with Serenity Tea and headed for the door.

He paused by the couch. "Feel better," he said, running a hand over Mica's messy hair. She knelt up and hugged him. When he tried to walk away she wouldn't let go. "I'd stay if I could…"

As he peeled her off, her arms went limp. "I know," she said. "Fun camp calls." He took two steps away from her, then came back. Maybe his aim was off, or maybe he was out of practice, but he kissed her eyebrow, then left. Everyone listened for the whine of a small motor pulling away.

"How's your stings?" Cody asked as the sound faded.

Mica kicked the scrambled sheets to the end of the couch, then turned her arm so she could see the angry trail. "Better."

"I dunno." Cody put his hands on his knees and got his face close to hers. "Your eye's all funny. It's like you're winking."

The lid was still pink and swollen. "It's no big deal," she said. "Let's see your sting, Ben."

"It's fine." I was pouring milk on cereal. "I can't even feel it." As I lowered my arm, my shirt chafed across the sting. It burned, but I didn't let on.

"You'd all better take it easy today," Mom said. "No more danger and excitement."

Just what I needed, another no-excitement day.

I helped Dad. Mica spent the day in the marina office with Mom, the two of them drawing and talking, until Cody stomped through complaining, "I am *so* bored. There is *so* nothing to do."

"Come on," Mica said. "I'll show you how to collect specimens for the aquariums."

Cody spent the rest of the day on the dock. He lay on his belly, dangling a line so thin it was almost invisible. The hair hook on the end was no bigger than a wasp stinger. For bait he used dead shrimp dipped off the top of the shrimp tank. Mica cut them in such tiny chunks that each one lasted a long, long time.

Cody pulled up the wrasses, grunts, damselfish, and sergeant majors that nibbled around the pilings. "Take a look at this one, Ben! Isn't it a beauty? It's so small!" It was like reverse fishing. He only threw the big ones back.

He caught enough to fill three aquariums. Of course Mica had to move things around. "Grunts by themselves," she said, dipping a net in the first tank. "Anything you put in with grunts croaks." That might be true. Or else Mica was lying. I never knew for sure when she lied, I only knew she did it.

The next day Cody said, "It hurts when I bend my knees." While he fished for specimens the sun had burned the backs of his legs.

"So, don't bend them," said Mica, who had come over for breakfast. She was around so much, my parents were probably beginning to think they had three kids.

"Do you guys feel up to a little trip?" Mom asked, putting a plate of whole wheat toast on the dinette.

Cody sat with his legs straight out. "A trip to where?" he asked.

"Key West. Dad and I thought that after your ordeal you kids might like to have some fun. Besides, we're leaving in a couple days. We need to do something spectacular."

"Me too?" Mica asked. "Can I come?"

"Of course, you too." Mom patted the top of her head. "I already cleared it with your father." Mica borrowed a pair of Mom's dark glasses. She said it was so no one could see her fat eye. Her eye looked fine to me—or close to fine. But she was getting all the mileage she could out of her stings.

We put the old Gone Fishin' sign in the window and piled into the ice-cream truck. The three of us shared the cot. Cody was being a pain. He still wouldn't bend his knees so he hogged most of the room.

Dad switched on the "Mary Had a Little Lamb" music as we crossed Snake Creek Bridge. Mica sang along, so Cody sang along. Then Mom and Dad had to chime in, Mom doing the high harmony.

I even sang a little—not so anyone could hear me, but it was a beautiful day. And, hey, we were driving all the way down the Overseas Highway to mile zero.

We hadn't even gotten through the town of Islamorada when Dad did a near-wheelie turning off the road into a sandy driveway. Three signs were posted. One said Helen Wadley Branch Library, another said County Park.

"AA," said Cody, reading the third one—the only sign he didn't have to sound out. "What's AA?"

There was a big silence in the front of the truck.

"Alcoholics Anonymous," said Mica. I couldn't see her eyes behind the dark glasses, but her voice sounded flat.

Dad swung the truck into a parking space. "You guys check out the park," he said. "Be back in a flash." As we climbed out he walked away whistling, like it was the most normal thing in the world for him to be going into a place called Alcoholics Anonymous.

Mica edged closer to me and lifted up on her toes. "Your dad has a problem, too?" she whispered.

"Yeah." Dad had a problem, but it wasn't drinking. His problem was that when he saw something going wrong, he butted in. It worked with his students sometimes. I had a feeling it wouldn't with Dr. Delano.

Cody wanted to try out the slide, but the metal was too hot for his legs. Mica sat on a swing, pushing herself back and forth with the toe of one flip-flop.

"Hey, Mica?" Cody said. "You wanna do double-Dutch?"

"Sure. What's double-Dutch?"

"Show ya," he said. "Stand on the seat."

Mica let her flip-flops drop in the dusty trough under the swing. "Just don't touch my sore arm," she warned, and stepped onto the seat. "Now what?"

"Now I stand on the seat going the other way and Ben pushes. Okay, Ben?"

I gave them a push.

"Hold the chain tight and lean back," Cody advised. "Now pump!" I noticed that his knees were working fine. The chains twisted until they got their knee-dipping and leaning synchronized, but by the time Dad came out of AA, pocket stuffed with brochures, Mica and my brother were sailing high, screeching with excitement. The biggest screams came when the swing hit the top of its arc and, just for a second, the chains went slack.

"Hey," said Dad. "Remember that time you and Cass did your big double-Dutch trick?"

"How could I forget?" I said. "You won't let me."

He winked. "Family legend."

It was about a million years ago. Cass and I were standing on the swing when she got her great idea. "I think we can fly, Ben," she whispered. "I know we can, if we let go at the exact right second." She didn't have to tell me what second she meant. It was the one when gravity stopped.

I wasn't so sure. I was already taking stuff apart with Dad. I knew that things worked, or didn't work, for a reason. If flying was that easy people would be doing it all the time. But Cass begged.

So we tried it. You could even say we flew a few feet before we crash-landed. I scraped both knees, both hands, my chin too. The swing hit Cass in the back of the head. She was so quiet after that, her mother kept checking to be sure her pupils were the same size. Cass had a goose egg, but she was okay. I think she was quiet because she was having a hard time getting used to the fact she couldn't fly.

"Poor Ben," said Dad, watching me watch Mica and my brother whoop it up. "Too old for double-Dutch and too young to drive."

"Yeah, Dad," I said. "It sucks."

We were on a bridge just south of Islamorada when Mica said, "See those posts?" They didn't look like much, just some twisted pieces of metal and broken concrete sticking out of the water. "That's part of the old Flagler Railroad," she said. "The whole thing got washed away in the 1935 hurricane."

"The train too?" Cody asked.

"Uh-huh, the train too."

"No way," he said. "A train is too heavy."

"Not for a hurricane." She hugged her knees. "You can't imagine how strong a hurricane is." From the way she said it, I knew that this time she wasn't bragging or lying. She was remembering.

The further we went down the Keys, the more water there was. Bridges got longer. When we hit the Seven Mile Bridge Dad asked, "Can anyone guess how long this bridge is?"

Cody thought it over, then sputtered, "Da-aad!"

We did a bunch of touristy things in Key West. We visited the sponge market. Mica impressed a couple of old guys in flower print shirts, along with their blue-haired wives, by reciting the Latin name for each sponge.

We ate conch fritters and Key lime pie. Mom insisted on seeing Ernest Hemingway's house. Mica and Cody spent most of the time patting the twelve-toed cats that lounged on the paths around the writer's house.

We stopped at a store called Fast Buck Freddie's that sold crazy things like mackerel squirt guns and singing alligators that worked on double-A batteries. I could have found my usual perfect gift for Cass there. Dad bought us all T-shirts that said Key Weird.

Cody complained we were wearing his legs out, so we rode the Conch Tour Train. Then he complained that the seat hurt his sunburn. "Tough," Mica said. Swaying along in the open cars, Mica slid right up against me. Then she looked the other way, pretending that she wasn't falling all over me. I put a hand on her shoulder and sat her back up, but as soon as we lurched around the next corner she fell right back against me. I guess it could have been an accident, but it happened over and over.

After the tour we made a john stop at the Kino Sandal Factory. "She likes you," Cody said as we peed.

"Who does?"

"Mica does."

"She likes you too," I said.

"Not *that* kind of like!" He sounded exasperated. "You know what I mean. *Like.*"

"That's sick," I said, zipping my fly. "She's eleven."

Driving home, Mica and Cody fell asleep, Cody with his head on her stomach. When Mica's toes brushed my leg I picked her foot up and moved it. Mom's sunglasses were half off her face. She looked goofy and really young. She wouldn't like to know it, but sleeping with her mouth open, she drooled.

Dr. Delano brought Mom shrimp, fresh off the dock. "See what you can do with these, Samantha Jean," he said. He called her by her full name. I thought only Dad did that. Mom made stir-fry. After dinner Dad and Dr. Delano went out on the porch so Dr. Delano could smoke a cigar. The rest of us stayed inside for dessert.

"Fruit salad?" Cody sounded disappointed. He'd been eating Mom's desserts all his life, but he still hoped for something that contained actual sugar.

I was chewing a bite of banana when Dr. Delano came back inside. His face was red. "Mica, we should be going now."

"But I haven't eaten my fruit—" Her dad silenced her with a look. "Okay, I'm coming." She slipped off the dinette bench. The Delanos marched out, stiff as the Coast Guard guys when they saluted the flag.

Dad sat back down and drummed his fingers on the table. "I probably blew that."

Mom picked up the Delanos' dishes and scraped the food they'd left onto one plate. "Want to dump this overboard for the fish, Cody?" As soon as my brother was out the door, she turned to Dad. "What did you say when you gave him the brochures? Were you subtle?"

"Forget subtle. We're leaving the day after tomorrow. The man needs to get ahold of himself," he said. "I'll kick his butt if I have to."

Mom put her arms around his neck. "I'm worried about her too."

"I'm not sure she's safe," he muttered, running a hand over Mom's arm.

I'd heard this conversation a hundred times before, although it was usually about one of Dad's students.

"What's wrong?" Cody asked, coming back inside with the empty plate. "You guys look all sad."

"They're worried about Mica," I told him. "But she's fine. She can take care of herself. And there are other things besides being safe."

"Sure there are," Dad replied. "But first you have to be safe."

"I have an idea," Cody chimed in. "Why don't we take Mica home with us."

"Now there's a solution, Samantha Jean." Dad turned to Mom with a smile. "The daughter you've always wanted!"

"Not funny, Dad," I said. "*Really* not funny."

chapter twenty-four

THE LAST SUNSET

O ur last day together," Mica said.
Cody swung his legs slowly. "Our last time of sitting on this picnic table."

"Our last sunset." Mica leaned back on her arms.

"Our last look at the baby grunts." Cody blinked at the blue-and-yellow striped fish he'd caught, then wiped his eyes with the back of his wrist.

Mica and Cody had been trading "lasts" all day. "Our last snorkel." "Our last lunch." "Our last time of fishing under the bridge."

Cody patted the glass on the grunt tank. "Bye bye, guys," he snuffed. All these lasts were getting to him.

The anemones in the first tank had just been fed. They hugged their dead-shrimp suppers with their inflato arms. The seahorses swam in the tank next to Mica. Their tiny fins moved quick as bees' wings. Each tank held something tropical, exotic—and way more interesting than Justin's goldfish, Xena.

I wasn't ready to go back to the land of goldfish yet. I was still waiting for something to happen—but we were running out of time.

We heard a big guffaw from inside the houseboat. Uncle Bert was back, along with his tiny wife, Aunt Emma. Mica had given both of them great big hugs when they arrived. "Well, if it isn't my little helper!" Aunt Emma had exclaimed.

Things changed the minute they got there. They made the houseboat seem small, and not ours anymore. For our last night aboard, me and Cody would be sleeping on the floor while Mom and Dad got our bunks.

"The food!" Uncle Bert boomed. From outside we could only hear Uncle Bert's part of the conversation. "My gosh, Mike, they had us eating all the time. I swear they woke us up in the middle of the night just so we could eat more. Look what they did to my boyish figure!"

Cody kicked at the bench. "How soon do you think we'll go see the fireworks, Ben?"

Uncle Bert was taking all of us out on the *Lazy Afternoon* to watch the fireworks being set off at Holiday Isle. "Don't rush it," I told him. "It's gotta get dark first."

"How about a last ride in the Zodiac?" Mica asked. "And a last fish in the creek?"

"Let's do it," I said, jumping down from the table. "You guys get the gear, I'll ask Dad." It felt better to be doing something, going somewhere, instead of sitting around wasting the last of our vacation. "Maybe we can find out what Mr. Trouble's up to tonight."

Dad tried to torpedo the last Zodiac trip. "I don't know, bud," he said. "It'll be dark soon. Maybe you kids should just stick around 'til it's time to go watch the fireworks."

"Come on, Mike!" Uncle Bert shouted. "You and Bobby used to shrimp half the night." Then he grabbed me by the back of the neck and lifted a little, like he was holding up the catch of the day. "Look here," he said, and he gave me a shake. "Benji's a big kid. Got a good head on his shoulders too. Let the kids go," he bellowed.

"Thanks, Uncle Bert!" I got out of there before Dad could overrule him.

We motored down the creek, stopping every once in a while to cast. The egrets and cormorants coming in for the night settled in the mangroves. As each new flock landed, the birds that were already there rattled their wings and poked the newcomers with their beaks.

"Hey, we were here first,'" Cody said in what he thought was a birdy voice. "This is *our* tree."

The clouds over the bay were turning pink and orange, changing the color of the creek. I dragged a hand through the water. Up home, the sun was setting too, sinking behind the line of trees at the end of our street. Miss Johnette and Anna were probably walking Beauty, and all the other dogs behind fences up and down the street were barking. This is *our* street, they were saying, just like the roosting birds claiming the mangroves. Bet Nana Grace is rocking back and forth in her chair on the porch, I thought. If it's chilly, she'll be wearing her old black sweater with the stretched-out pockets. I could almost hear the creak of the rocker and the sound of her humming. Then, figuring that Justin and Clay got scooters for Christmas too, I added the sound of wheels.

I saved Cass for last. Where was she? On the sofa, watching TV with her folks? Hanging with Jemmie? But then I saw her, clear as anything. She was by herself, sitting in her chair behind the bush, and she was looking up, hunting for the first star so she could wish on it. I knew some of the things Cass wished for: a room of her own, fewer freckles, college, the Olympics. But maybe she sometimes made a wish with my name in it, maybe tonight. I hunted around for that same first star. It was still pretty light, but I found it and wished, I won't say for what, but her name was in it.

"Are you fishing or snoozing?" Mica asked. I shagged a cast up under the mangroves, tucking it in between two roots.

"Perfect," said Cody. "The last perfect cast."

"Like fun it is," Mica said. "Watch this one, junior." She put her shrimp down just inches from mine. "Your turn, Cody. Make it three for three."

Cody reared back. He put so much into that cast, he grunted. "All right!" I yelled. His plug was headed for the sweet spot at the edge of the mangroves.

Maybe the wind gave his plug a push, but it came down a few feet back in the thicket of branches. We could see it swinging among the leaves, winking orange in the setting sun. Cody slumped. "Oh, man..." He passed me the rod.

"Tough break," I told him. I tried to snap the lure out of the mangroves, but it must've wrapped itself around a branch. The trees shook a little, then the line broke.

Cody laid his rod across his knees and sighed again. "The last lost lure."

Mr. Trouble must've been busy somewhere else. We never even got a last bite. Our last Zodiac trip was just a ride down the creek and back, and now it was over. We idled at the mouth of the canal. "You brothers want to do a first?" Mica asked quietly.

"Sure," I said. After piling up so many "lasts," a first sounded good to me. "What do you have in mind?"

"Let's take the Zodiac under the bridge, just a little ways, so we can look back and see the sunset over the islands. What do you say, brothers?"

Cody shook his head. "Dad told us not to go under the bridge."

"Technically true," Mica admitted. "But *why* did he say it? Because he thinks we'll get in trouble. *We* know we won't. We're only going for a few measly minutes. It's not like we'll get caught or anything."

I heard Uncle Bert's belly laugh all the way down the canal. The adults were in the houseboat sipping iced tea, chatting; they'd never even know. Through the bridge was the wide Atlantic Ocean. "Okay," I said. "Let's do it."

"But Dad said—"

"We can put you out on the dock," I told my brother, "but I'm going. So, how about it? Are you in?"

Cody swallowed hard, then nodded.

As we passed the huge concrete pilings, I thought how small the Zodiac was. But we'd be okay. Five minutes out, five minutes back. What could happen?

The wind had been blowing from bay to ocean all day. According to Uncle Bert, the winter wind normally blew inshore. "Must be catching the edge of a nor'easter," he had said. As soon as we broke out into the open, the wind began to push us.

"How far are we going?" Cody asked, looking back at the bridge longingly.

"Just out of the channel," said Mica.

Good, I thought. Open water. The well-marked channel was about as exciting as our street back home.

With the wind helping the motor, we moved faster than we ever had on Snake Creek. We blew by the red and green triangles and squares of the channel markers and past the head pin. I held out the sides of my windbreaker; Mica did the same with her cover-up. We became sails.

"Water's getting deep," Cody reported. "I can't see the bottom! Guys…" But me and Mica were watching the horizon, listening to the snap of our jackets in the wind.

"Far enough!" said Cody, and he shoved the handle Mica had let go of when she turned herself into a sail. We circled until we faced shore. Now the breeze was in our faces. It felt cool on my eyeballs. It pushed my shirt flat against my chest. The windows of the bridge tender's station were on fire in the sunset. The two islands the bridge joined, Windley and Plantation, already looked dark. But the clouds above were lit with reds and oranges. A line of cormorants straggled across the sky.

Cody tugged Mica's arm. "Can we go back now?"

"In a second." She turned the Zodiac again. "We have to take one last look at the ocean." If she was thinking what I was thinking, she was ready to keep heading out, to go where the wind would take us for just a little longer.

"Okay," said Cody. "Enough looking."

"Hey," Mica said, squinting to cut the shine. "What's that?"

"What's what?" I squinted too.

"Over there, Ben, you see it? Something white. What do you think it is?"

"Can't tell," I said. "Want to check it out?"

"No!" Cody hugged his PFD. "I wanna go back in!"

"You know, it could be something valuable," Mica told him.

"Like more tools?" he mumbled.

"We'll take a quick look, then head in," I assured him. For the record, I didn't think we were going to find anything valuable—I don't believe in the tooth fairy or Santa Claus either—but I wanted to make the trip last. Our next trip oceanside we'd be crowded in the *Lazy Afternoon* with the adults. Uncle Bert or Dad would drive. The three of us would be nothing but kids along for the ride.

We chased the pale shape. Whatever it was, the wind was pushing it too, so it took a while before we pulled alongside. The white Styrofoam rectangle bobbed.

"Just an old cooler lid," Cody said. "I told you guys."

Hanging out under the lid were a couple dozen small fish. We all leaned over the side to see them. For the first time I noticed that, dead in the water, we were chopping up and down, landing after each short wave with a slap. "Time to head in," I said. We all sat up and looked back toward shore. For a few seconds nobody said anything.

"What happened?" Cody whispered. "How'd we get out so far?"

The lights of the bridge were tiny, and the orange path of fading sunlight that ran between us and the bridge seemed awful long.

"Big deal," Mica said. "We went a little farther than we meant to. I'll have you back safe and sound before you know it, Cody."

The motor buzzed. It was a splashy trip as the Zodiac bucked the chop. "Are we moving?" Cody asked after a while.

"Of course we are." Mica sounded put out. "We're fighting the wind, so it'll take a little longer."

"But it'll be *dark* soon," Cody said.

"Great. Cody's afraid of the dark," Mica said.

"Don't worry," I told him. "It gets dark every night. Nothing ever happens. Besides, I bet we'll make it before it gets really dark."

Mica and Cody, even the gray rubber Zodiac, were painted

orange. We could just see where the sun touched the water and dissolved under the bridge. It was beautiful, but scary-beautiful. Soon it would be as dark as the inside of your sleeve.

We went a while longer, but the bridge seemed almost as far away as ever. "I'm cold," Cody whimpered.

"Don't whine," Mica scolded. "I'll have you back to civilization in a minute."

Maybe not in a minute, but I still thought we'd get there.

Cody stared at the bridge like he could pull us in quicker if he concentrated. "Dad'll kill us for sure."

"We'll tell him we hijacked you," I said. I looked around for something to distract him. "Hey, Cody, there's the first star."

"First planet," Mica corrected. Then she softened. "Go on, Cody, make a wish."

"I wish I was home," Cody blurted out.

"Here home, or home, home?" I asked.

"All the way home, on my own street, in my own house, in my own room, in my own bed."

I looked up at the star/planet, which had risen some since I'd wished on it. Tomorrow I'd see Cass. I wondered what she thought of the necklace. She probably thought her buddy Ben had really lost it. I remembered my wish—but if a wish made things okay with Cass, would it be the same? Maybe there are some things you can't wish for.

Besides, it might take more than Cody's wish to get us in to shore. I canceled my first wish and threw mine in on top of his. I didn't want to be all the way home and tucked in our beds, but I wouldn't mind being back to where we could hear Uncle Bert's laugh.

Cody wrestled his arms through the armholes to the inside of his PFD. "It's really cold out here." He looked like he was wearing a straitjacket. "We're getting closer, right?"

"Of course we are," said Mica. The bridge tender's tower looked a little bigger, but not much. I began to wonder how long I'd be grounded for. One week? Two?

Cody was quiet a minute. "We're not getting any closer," he whispered. "We're staying in one place. It's just the same waves over and over. I recognize them."

"The same waves!" Mica was laughing at him when the motor died. Without that reassuring buzz, her laughter sounded strange and hollow. She cut the laugh short. We all stared at the motor.

"Ben?" Cody's voice was small. "You can fix it, can't you?"

"Move, Mica. Let me take a look." I was already pretty sure I knew what was wrong, but I checked anyway. "The good news is that nothing's broke," I said, sitting back on my heels. "The bad news is we're out of gas."

"Out of gas? We can't be." Mica picked up the red plastic gas tank and shook it. It didn't slosh. "I don't get it. We had plenty when we left the dock!"

"Well, we don't any more. Not even fumes."

Cody opened his mouth and let out a wail, followed by an even louder one.

"Stop it!" Mica scolded. "Just zip it. Your brother and I have to think."

Cody zipped, but every now and then a sob got out.

Without the motor to fight it, the wind pushed the Zodiac like a paper cup across a puddle. That's when I began to think we might be in trouble. But I didn't let it show. "Any ideas, Mica? I'm open to all suggestions."

"First thing is, we should steer the boat with the motor," Mica said.

"But the motor's not working!" Cody cried.

"I know that. But we can still use it as a rudder to run downshore."

"We need to go back to the marina," he sniffled. "We need to go back *now!*"

"One thing at a time," I told him as I turned the dead motor. "The first thing is to make sure we don't end up sending Mom and Dad a postcard from Cuba."

"I don't want to send a postcard from Cuba!"

"Forget Cuba," said Mica. "If we blow out far enough we'll get into the Gulf Stream, and it'll take us north. If we wash up anywhere it'll be up the coast, like Fort Lauderdale, maybe."

Cody snuffed. "Is that better or worse than Cuba?"

"It's better," I said. "Way better. Mom and Dad could drive up and get us. Plus, they speak English in Fort Lauderdale."

But what if we didn't fetch up against anything? What if all we ever saw again was water? Think, I told myself. You've got to think. If the engine was broke I could have come up with something. All those nights and weekends of working with Dad, I had learned you could usually rig something. A temporary something, maybe, but all we had to do was get back to Bert's Marina.

I took a quick inventory of everything we had aboard: fishing rods, twenty feet of rope, a tackle box, a bait bucket, an emergency kit including snakebite supplies, a flashlight and a flare, oars, and three cold kids in PFDs—one so scared he was about to pee his pants. "Don't worry, Cody. Me and Mica'll get you back in." I didn't think of it as a lie exactly. Dad had told me to look out for my brother. Keeping him from getting scared was part of the job.

The lights onshore were getting smaller. Steering with the motor we were following the shore, but still angling slightly away. I lashed an oar to the motor so it worked better as a rudder. "Great," I said. "We're following the shore. Now all we need is a plan to get back in." I knew Cody wasn't thinking of a way to get us in. When things get tough, Cody turns back into a little kid. But Mica seemed to have quit too. I couldn't afford to have her crap out on me.

"I'm surprised an old hand like you can't come up with something, Mica." Her silhouette sat up stiff. "I mean, you've lost a mast in a gale. Even if you could only think of a way we could stay put, that would be something. There's no anchor, right?"

"Sure there's an anchor. I have one up my butt."

Usually Cody would laugh himself sick about an anchor up somebody's butt. All he did was wipe his runny nose on the shoulder of his PFD and say, "I don't want to go to Fort Lauderdale."

"We're going back to Bert's Marina," I said. "Mica's coming up with something."

My brother gripped her shoulder. "When all else fails, think."

"I *am* thinking." She shrugged the hand off. "The tide was coming in when we left Snake Creek, wasn't it?" she asked.

I wouldn't have known when we first got to Bert's Marina, but hanging out with her I had begun to notice things like that. Now I remembered that the blades of floating turtle grass on the surface had been drifting slowly toward the bay. "That's right, in."

"We could put out a sea anchor," she said. "If we had one."

"What's a sea anchor?" Cody asked.

"It's something you hang over the side, like a bucket. The wind is blowing out now, but the tide is going in. The bucket catching the water would hold us in one place. Or at least slow us down."

"Great idea," I said. "How about this?" I grabbed the bait bucket with its small perforated door. A bucket with a wide-open top would've been better, but hey, you work with what you have.

"Fat lot of good that'll do," Mica said. But I ignored her.

I was about to drop it over the side when Cody nudged me with his bare toes. "Let the shrimp go first."

It crossed my mind that we might need the shrimp later. To eat. Or for bait to catch the fish we'd eat raw. It sounded gross now, but it might sound better by day two.

Or day three.

Or day twelve.

"Ben?" My brother was waiting.

I pushed the bait bucket door. Our future food spilled over the side.

"Good luck, guys," Cody said, waving at them.

"They don't stand a chance," Mica said. "Things have big teeth out here."

"Like…Jaws? Remember when Jaws bit the boat, Ben?" He was

reliving the scene of the Great White taking a bite out of a boat a lot bigger than our Zodiac.

"Good going, Mica. Scare him to death." I tossed the bucket in the water. It bobbed, then rolled, taking on water. It was only half submerged when it quit filling and stopped, line tight, between us and the bridge. "How come it won't sink?" I asked.

"It's a trolling bucket," Mica said. "It's designed to *not* sink."

"Still, it's helping," I said. "Feel the drag?" I was excited. "What else? What else can we tow behind us?"

"Your brother?" Mica suggested, and he let out a muffled sob. "Just kidding, Cody." She put an arm around his shoulders.

Cody snuffed. "How about the tackle box? Could we throw that over?"

"Good thinking!" Mica dumped the tackle out and tied the handle to a line. There was another splash. The box floated a little, then turned turtle and sank.

We still had one oar, but I thought we might need it later. Short of towing my brother, we'd done all we could.

It was hard to judge. Except for a couple of the brighter lights the shore had about disappeared, but it seemed like we were going slower. For one thing, the motion of the boat was different. We had stopped skimming along. Now we rose, then dropped. Each wave slap sent spray over the bow. It drummed the rubber like a heavy rain.

"Ben?" Cody said. "I'm feeling kind of barfy."

"Do like Dr. Delano said. Watch the horizon. Don't take your eyes off the lights."

"Is that Fort Lauderdale over there?"

"No," said Mica. "Islamorada. We won't head for Ft. Lauderdale until the Gulf Stream picks us up."

Until? I thought.

Cody pointed. "But that's our bridge, right?"

"No, that's the bridge at Whale Harbor." Beneath the bridge was a smudge of pink, the last of the last sunset we'd come out to see. The headlights of cars crossing the bridge were tiny.

"It's getting really dark," Cody murmured.

"But that's good, because now if we signal with a light someone will see it. Right, Mica?"

"Yeah, maybe." She slowly pulled out the flashlight and the emergency flare.

I took the flashlight out of her hand. "Here. You hold it, Cody. Be ready to signal if you see a boat."

He just sat there.

"Give it here," Mica said. "Cody's being a baby."

"Am not!" He squirmed a hand out the bottom of his PFD and took the flashlight.

"You be ready to use that," I said. "There are going to be people coming out to watch the fireworks from the water. When they do, you signal them, okay? You do that, and they'll come get us."

"For really?" he asked.

"For really." We all turned toward the bridge and watched for boats to come through and rescue us. But there weren't any. The spray across the bow soaked us again. I could hear Cody's teeth chattering. "Come sit over by me," I told him.

Cody was on his way back to the stern when Mica shouted, "Look, brothers!" A spot of light had appeared beneath the bridge. Cody fumbled to turn on the flashlight, but Mica said, "Wait. Switch it on when he gets closer so it'll catch his attention."

"Quick. Get your arm out so you can wave the light around," I told him.

Cody twisted around like an escape artist. Out came an arm. "Ready, Freddie," he said.

The few strands of hair that weren't soaked whipped around Mica's face. She held them back with one hand and watched the boat's headlight grow. "All right, Cody. NOW!"

He pressed the button and waved the light.

"Whoa, Cody," I said. "Shine that toward me a second. Oh, man…" The bulb was barely lit. "Battery's going dead. You check your equipment out, Mica?"

"Don't look at me. I changed the batteries last week. It's the salt air. It corrodes everything."

"You changed them last week?"

"Well..." Mica wouldn't look at me. "Almost last week."

Cody shook the flashlight. The filament in the bulb flickered, then died. "Please, please, see us," he whispered, staring at the boat we'd been trying to signal. "Please, please, please." The boat turned away.

We had been *that* close to a ride back to shore. I turned on Mica. "*Almost* last week? What does that mean exactly? Last month? Last year?"

"Why are you yelling at me?" she shouted back. "You're the oldest! You should've said, 'Dumb idea, Mica,' when I suggested going under the bridge. You're supposed to look out for Cody."

"Oh yeah? My dad put you in charge of him when we're on the water, remember?"

"Stop it, you two, stop!" Cody screamed. "I don't want either one of you in charge of me!" And he hurled the flashlight into the sea.

chapter twenty-five

ADRIFT

We felt a *thump, thump, thump.* The Zodiac quivered.

"Jaws!" my brother screamed.

"Hold off, Cody," I said. "We don't know what hit us." It came again: *thump, thump.*

"Jaws," he whispered. "We're all gonna die." I could tell he was crying.

"Hush up, Cody," Mica snapped. "If it was Jaws we'd be dead already. It's just the sea anchor dragging bottom."

Cody hiccuped. "I thought we were out in the ocean, way deep."

"Sure, most of the time," she said. "But the bottom shoals up in places."

Thump, thump.

"Hey, if anything is sticking up from the bottom the open box might snag on it, or the rope might catch. Then we could tie up." I threw myself down and grabbed the rope to the tackle box. I was freezing in my soaked clothes, but the water lapping my arms was warm as I swung the rope.

Mica threw herself down too. I shoved her with my elbow when she tried to take the rope out of my hands. I felt a couple of shocks as the sea anchor dragged over the bottom, but it didn't hang up on anything. In a minute we were adrift in deep water again.

The two of us sat up. "Should've let me do it," Mica said.

"How would that've helped? Do you have X-ray vision?" I looked over at my scared little brother. "Don't worry, bro. We'll hook something next time. Okay?"

"I can't see shore." Cody sounded panicky. "And I can't see Cuba. All I see is water."

Suddenly, there was a burst of light from the shore followed by a muffled *boom!* The first of the fireworks had been set off at Holiday Isle. "You think Mom and Dad are there, watching?" he asked.

"Mom and Dad are looking for us, Cody."

"Really?" He cheered up for about two seconds. "Will they find us?"

"Of course they'll find us." I sounded way more positive than I felt.

"Realistically?" Mica said. "Realistically, I'd give it a fifty-fifty chance."

"Half yes, half no?"

"Mica, that's enough." I slid over by Cody and put my arm around him. I hated the way his shoulders felt so hunched up and scrawny. I wished I *had* put him out on the dock. "Listen, bro. We're gonna be fine. Have I ever lied to you?"

He shook his head, no.

"And do you think I'd start now?"

I squeezed his shoulder and he shook his head again.

"So when I say we're going to get found, you believe me, okay?"

"Yeah. Okay."

"All right! Slap me five, bro!" Normally, Cody could make my palm sting, but his hand was wet and slippery. Besides, this time I wasn't so sure he believed me.

"I'm not saying we won't get found," Mica put in. "We probably will, like Ben says. Lucky thing we're in a Zodiac. Explorers have taken them thousands of miles."

"Is Fort Lauderdale more than thousands of miles away?"

"You kidding? Fort Lauderdale is only about this far." She snapped her fingers. "Zodiacs have crossed the Atlantic. So we're safe...unless we never get found."

"What are you trying to do, Mica?" My voice sounded high, like about sixth grade.

"I'm giving him the straight scoop, Ben. The truth."

"You could've picked a better time to start doing that." The bow took a harsh slap and we all got drenched.

Mica wiped her face with the sleeve of her cover-up. "Are you saying I lie?"

"Like a rug!"

Cody rocked against me. "Mom'll be so sad. She'll never see her boys again." He was making himself cry, thinking about the dead-and-gone boys who happened to be us. "And what about your mom, Mica? Bet she'll be sorry she spent all that time dancing."

"Yeah…well…" Mica twisted her wet hair back. "I don't think she'll even know. And if she does, I guess she won't care."

"What do you mean? Of course she will. She'll come and throw flowers on the water. Both our moms will."

As soon as Cody found out that the little roadside wreaths marked places where fatal car wrecks had happened, he asked Mom, "If I was in a crash, and if I died, you'd put a wreath at the very spot, wouldn't you?" Then he bugged her until she promised. Now he had both our mothers boo-hooing and scattering flowers.

My throat hurt. The thing was, I could see Mom doing it. She'd take the flower from behind her ear and drop it on our watery graves.

Mica was very quiet. Uncharacteristically quiet. Blue and orange fireworks opened like beach umbrellas behind her. She hugged herself, her wet arms forming a complicated knot. "It's really just the Captain and me," she said at last. *Boom, boom!*

"What about your mother on tour?" She didn't answer Cody. "You don't *have* a mother?" he asked, leaning toward her.

"Of course I have a mother. To not have a mother is biologically impossible. But I don't *have* her. Not like you have yours."

"What about the ring? If it isn't your mother's, whose is it?"

"It's hers, but it's not like she gave it to me. She screwed it off her finger and threw it in the driveway. The Captain wanted to back the Jeep over it, but I picked it up and put it on a chain for safekeeping."

"Safekeeping for what?" Cody asked.

"For when she came back. I was sure she would, and then everything would be like before."

"When they got along," Cody added.

"Who said they got along? They fought all the time. My mother threw things. My father slammed doors and yelled. But they always got back together. Those were the best times. It was like…" Mica looked up, trying to think of something it was like. "You know how you feel when you have to throw up and you just want it over with? That's what it was like before a fight. But after a fight, when they got back together, it was like the feeling you get right after you upchuck. All calm and quiet and relieved."

Cody, the easy-barfer, nodded. But I thought things would have to be pretty bad to make throwing up seem good.

"That's the way it always was, until the last time," she said. "My grandmother said she went off with somebody else. After that, the Captain hated to be around the house. When he got his next grant we moved aboard the *Martina*. We've been traveling ever since."

"That isn't even her real name, is it?" Cody, who had believed Mica's story completely, now must've figured every part of it was a lie.

"No. My mother's name is *Martina*, just like I said."

"But if she dumped him, why's her name still on your boat?" I asked.

"You don't know anything, Ben Floyd. You are beyond clueless." A silver shower of sparks lit the sky behind her. "He still loves her is why."

"Come on," I said. It was like out of the soap operas Cass's sister, Lou, watched.

"If we don't make it in alive he'll have to find her and tell her," Cody said. "Maybe that would get them back together."

That's exactly what would happen on one of Lou's soaps.

"They're going to have to get back together on their own," I said. "No way we're going to die. No way." I went back to scanning the water for a moving light. Maybe Mica's life isn't so great after all, I thought. For a second I almost felt sorry for her.

"I don't want to die," Cody whimpered. "Grandpa died. I guess I'd see him in heaven."

"If there is a heaven," Mica said.

"Will you shut up! We're not about to find out," I said. But hard as I stared, there was nothing coming under the bridge. I'd screwed up. Big time. On the ocean the Zodiac was not much more than the floating cooler lid, but it was all there was between us and the black water. I was really scared. I turned and looked out to sea, trying to find anything that wasn't water or sky.

That's when I saw it. "Look! A light!" I figured that the blinking light belonged to a boat, anchored out. It was still a ways off, but I cupped my hands around my mouth and yelled, "Hey!" as loud as I could.

Mica turned. "Don't bother yelling," she said. "That's not a boat. It's some kind of marker." She leaned forward, arms still wrapped around herself. "You know what I think? I think it's the tower on Hens and Chickens. Brothers, if we can get over to it we can tie up."

"You mean we might not die?" Cody asked.

"Looks like you're going to see your seventh birthday after all," I said.

Cody's seventh birthday was no done deal, but if we could tie up to the tower we had a real chance. I began to wonder again how long I'd be grounded for.

The way the wind was blowing, it would take us *past* the metal tower, not *to* it. I jerked the second oar out of its holder and dug it into the water. I tried like mad to change course. "Come on, guys, use your hands," I urged. There was no time to untie the oar we were using as a rudder.

Cody and Mica shoveled with their hands, I skulled with the oar, and we turned toward the marker. But not fast enough. We were going to miss it by a good fifty feet, blow right by. "Mica, it's time for that perfect cast of yours."

Mica sat up. "What? Oh…I get it." She grabbed her rod. I knew she had a grouper plug on, a big lure, with three treble hooks—and that she could cast as well as any guy I knew. Let her hook the tower, I thought. I'll deal with her bragging later.

The plug sailed…and landed with a splash, way to the left of the tower. "Wind got it," she said, taking up line fast.

Cody picked up his rod. "Maybe I can hook it. I hooked a mangrove." But his short cast splashed down a few feet from the Zodiac.

My shoulders burned from paddling, but it was no use. We were coming even with the tower but not to it. Soon we would pass it, our one chance gone. "Quick, Mica. Try again."

Mica's second cast hit one of the tower's metal legs. We were cheering but then we heard the lure splash into the water. Mica didn't waste a second before reeling in, but by the time she got the line in it would be too late. I threw the oar down on the floor of the Zodiac, reached over Cody, and snatched up my own rod. We had just passed the tower. I stood to cast. It was the only way to get enough power.

The Zodiac yawed. Mica threw her weight the other way. Cody latched onto my ankles. "Sit down, Ben, you're gonna go overboard!" But I was completely focused. I had one cast. There wouldn't be a second chance.

The fishing rod whistled as I whipped it back, then forward. The lure flew. Like Mica's, it clattered against the metal superstructure. But this time I felt the Zodiac hesitate, pinned to one place in the water. I felt the line pull. "Got it!" I yelled. Cody cheered, Mica cheered.

Then the line broke.

"No!" I shouted. I sat down hard and dropped my head onto my folded arms. Cody started crying. About now would be a good time to say something reassuring, I thought. But I couldn't do it.

Head down, I thought of Cass. How will she feel if I die? Pretty bad, I guess. Not because she's in love with me or anything, but just because I've been there her whole life.

I felt a stab in my throat and swallowed hard. Bet the guys would feel bad too. Word would get around at school. For a while everyone at Monroe Middle would talk about me, the kid who drowned over

Christmas break. They'd have a memorial assembly, and dedicate a bench or something. Cass and Jemmie and Anna, Justin, Clay, and Leroy. All of them would grow up, but not me. I'd never get my license. I'd never get tall.

Cody's snuffles were getting louder. Mica was doing her own brand of comforting. "What did you expect, Cody? That was really a long shot. Like maybe a one-in-five chance."

"Are we going to die?" Cody asked.

Even if we *were* going to die I couldn't sit there and let him be scared. I lifted my head off my arms. "We're going to be—"

The Zodiac jerked. "A fish!" Cody yelled, and his rod tip bent down hard. After his sorry attempt at casting on the tower he had left his line trailing in the water.

Mica dropped to her knees and leaned over the side. "You caught the rope of a lobster trap."

"What?" Then I saw the Styrofoam buoy, pulled hard against the side of the Zodiac. Cody had hooked the rope that went from the marker to the trap. "Good work, Cody!" I pounded his back.

Mica lashed us to the trap's buoy line to be sure we were secure. As we all high-fived, the fireworks at Holiday Isle reached the grand finale. *Boom, boom!* We pounded each other and shouted, "Happy New Year!" It was like the end of a movie. Flashing lights. Lots of sound. So what if we were way offshore? So what if no one knew where we were? It was just a matter of time before we would be found.

Maybe I still had a shot at growing up to be taller than Leroy.

chapter twenty-six

IF WE NEVER GET RESCUED

The Zodiac tugged at the rope, the same motion over and over and over. Cody was crying again. He was quiet about it, but I could feel the sobs shake him.

"We n-n-need to c-c-conserve heat." Mica's chattering teeth chopped the words. "We n-n-eed to g-g-get c-close." The three of us squeezed together on the seat, Cody on one side of me, Mica on the other.

Cody put his head in my lap, stuck his thumb in his mouth, and fell asleep. "Cody still sucks his thumb?" Mica whispered.

"Not for a couple of years now. He's kind of stressed." I didn't mention seeing her pink, wrinkled thumb.

She shivered hard against me. It felt kind of funny, but I put my arm around her shoulders. That didn't stop the shaking. "You okay?" I asked.

"My hands are n-numb," she said. "I can't feel them."

"Jeez!" I yelped as she shoved them under my PFD. "Stay on your own side of the shirt, okay?"

Her hands slid out from under my shirt, but stayed inside my life vest. "You weren't kidding," I gasped. "Your hands are like ice."

When she tucked her head under my chin, I noticed that her hair didn't have a girl smell like soap. It smelled tangy.

"Let's talk," she said.

"About what?" I asked, wary. If she was going to tell me she *liked* me, I was trapped.

She sighed. "Tell me more about your neighborhood."

"My neighborhood?" That was a relief. "Okay. What about it?"

"Like things that happened."

She snuggled against me, burrowing into my chest. "Would you cut that out!"

"Cut what out?" She pulled away, her eyes catching the shine of moonlight. "You don't think I *like* you, do you? Yuck! I don't want to die of hypothermia is all, and you're the only source of heat out here. Now tell me about the neighborhood."

I felt pretty stupid. If my body heat helped her out, she was welcome to it. Besides, I was cold too. Real cold. I thought back to summer, trying to come up with a warm story. "There's this place at the edge of the neighborhood where the power lines go through. It's back behind a little strip of woods, so it's hard to see from the houses. Me and Justin, Clay and Leroy—the guys I told you about—built a bike racetrack out there. We had the highest jumps and the deepest pits." I tried to remember being so hot sweat trickled inside my shirt and soaked the hair under my helmet. "Me and Clay went head to head. We about killed each other."

"I'd like to see you race s-s-sometime."

"The track's not there anymore. We had to cover it when dumb Clay went and broke his arm." I tried to feel the heat, but the only heat was Mica, breathing into my chest. It reminded me of when Cody fell asleep against me on long trips and breathed a wet spot onto my shirt.

"What about the girls?" She hugged me around the ribs. "Not Cass. Tell me about one of the other ones."

"There's Jemmie and Anna." But I couldn't talk about Jemmie without mentioning Cass. "Anna's pretty new in the neighborhood. When she got there she was a foster kid. She'd been passed around a lot. She brought a collection of rocks with her. One from each place she'd lived."

"I do that too!" Mica sounded excited. "Only with shells. I pick up a shell in each place we stay. Do you think she'd like to see them sometime?"

"Sure, why not?" I couldn't tell where we were going with this. Mica and Anna lived in separate worlds. It wasn't like they were about to meet. But I played along. "She's kind of like you. You know, scientific. This fall Anna and Miss Johnette—she's the lady Anna lives with now—did a botanical survey of the neighborhood. They made a list of every kind of weed that grew in everybody's lawn. Jemmie told Anna, 'Girl, that may be a specimen to you, but to me it's just a beggar-tick plant. About all they're good for is stickin' to your socks.'" Freezing to death and lost at sea, we laughed.

Her hair tickled my neck as she looked up. "If I wrote Anna a letter and sent it home with you, do you think she'd answer?"

"Where would she mail the answer to? You don't have a mailbox."

"Mica Delano, care of Bert's Marina."

"How long'll you be there?"

I felt Mica shrug. "Another couple of weeks. I'd get it if she wrote right away."

"She'd write." I'd tell Anna how lonely Mica was. Anna knew about being lonely. Once they started writing, they'd get to like each other. They were both adventurous, basically nice—and basically weird.

Cody whimpered in his sleep and pulled his legs up tight to his chest. "It's okay, Cody." Mica slid her hand out from under my life jacket and stroked his hair. "Hush, you'll be fine." She was doing Mom, telling him the same things Mom had told her when she got stung by the man-of-war.

My eyes were already raw from the salt spray, but now they felt hot. I blinked hard, thinking I might not see Mom again.

"Hey, look at that. The moon's full."

"Nuh-uh." She tipped her head back against my shoulder. "It won't be full for two more days."

Here we were, lost at sea, about to have people toss flowers on the ocean for us, and she *still* had to be right.

The water in the bottom sloshed over my bare feet, making a sound each time the craft jerked against the rope. If the wave was big, a little more lapped over. Sometimes we felt the lobster trap skip across the bottom, towed by the Zodiac. I was having a hard time keeping my eyes open. "Wake me up when I'm dead," I told her.

I must have dozed off, because when I opened my eyes the moon was higher in the sky. What woke me up was the distant sound of an engine. The others were still asleep but, thanks to Dad, I was tuned in to that kind of noise. "Mica, wake up! Cody!" I jostled them. "Wake up, you guys!" Mica's warm, wet breath quit hitting my neck. Cody sat up, rubbing his eyes. We all listened. The engine sound was faint, but getting louder. It was coming our way.

A beam of light swept across the water. "A searchlight!" Mica said. "Someone's looking for us."

"Over here!" Cody yelled at the top of his lungs. "We're over here!" He waved his arms. I had to grab the butt of his shorts to keep him from falling overboard.

"They can't hear you, Cody."

"Mom!" he screamed.

Mica was digging in the metal box that held the emergency supplies. The snakebite kit splashed to the floor, followed by the Band-Aids and the gauze. "Here's the flare gun," she said. "We only have one flare, so we can't mess up."

"Shoot it," said Cody. "Shoot it, now!" He looked at her then me, not sure who was in charge.

Mica and I stared at each other. "What do you think?" she asked. "Wait?"

"If we only have one, I say wait."

Things got real quiet aboard the Zodiac. We watched the searchlight pan across the water. Cody pounded my thigh with his fists when the boat turned away. "Told you she should've shot it!"

What he hadn't figured out was that the boat was tacking back and forth, covering a wide area. The light was getting bigger with each pass.

"What if they give up and go in?" my brother asked. "What if?"

Mica held the flare gun in both hands.

"Now?" she asked, raising the gun over her head.

"Not yet. Wait 'til the light is shining right at us. Then we'll know they're looking this way."

Cody sobbed. The light was running parallel to shore, heading away. "They'll never find us now." But the progress of the light slowed. The beam swung until the line of light was an arrow pointing toward us.

I yelled, "Now, Mica!"

The flare left the Zodiac with a whoosh and a blinding flash. Cody coughed and fanned the air. "It stinks like somebody cut one!"

Smoked in, we heard something that made us hug each other and shout. The hum of the boat's engine had jumped an octave. Whoever it was had seen our flare and they were coming as fast as they could push the engine.

The light got bigger and bigger and after a while we could see the black shape of the boat against the moon. The sport fisherman came down off plane and slowed. Whoever it was knew about Hens and Chickens and didn't want to run aground. A skinny silhouette lurched out onto the bow. The beam of a handheld search lamp poured across the water.

"Captain!" Mica yelled. "Over here!"

"Mica? Oh, thank God." Dr. Delano's voice was full of tears and relief.

"Ben, Cody, are you boys there?" It was my father's voice. I felt like my heart would bust.

"We're here!" Cody yelled, and they idled over to us.

As they pulled alongside, Mica's father leaned over the bow rail and grabbed her hands. "I was afraid you were gone too." With his strong arms, he lifted her out of the raft and crushed her to his chest. "Gone, just like her."

He was crying, Mica was crying. "I wouldn't do that to you," she sobbed. "Never, ever." They held onto each other like they were the last two people on earth.

My father swept Cody and me up, one with each arm. "Boys!" he shouted. "Ben. I told you not to go out oceanside. What if we hadn't found you?" He hugged us hard, then held us out by our shoulders. "God! What would I have told your mother?"

"Where *is* Mom?" Cody choked out as Dad squeezed the air out of both of us again. "Did she go to the fireworks?"

"Of course she didn't go. She's on the Coast Guard boat looking for you, and she's scared out of her wits."

I felt lousy. Why didn't I think? I know how scared Mom can get. "Sorry, Dad. I screwed up."

"You sure did." He hugged me again.

"I want Mom," Cody whimpered. "And can we get something to eat? I'm starving."

Dad radioed the Coast Guard. They put Mom on. "Mike, do you have the boys?"

"Safe and sound," he said. There was a long silence, then I heard my mother crying. It was the worst sound I ever heard.

Heading in, Mica wore her father's jacket, and Cody wore Dad's. Since there wasn't a third one handy, I said I didn't need one. I stood at the helm where the windshield and console cut the wind, right beside Dad. No one heard my teeth chattering over the noise of the engine. The Zodiac, tied behind, bounced along on our wake.

chapter twenty-seven

WE RIDE!

The sun was barely up, but we were out on the dock in our swimsuits. I guess it was stupid after spending half the night on the water, freezing, but we wanted to sneak in one last swim before going.

It was just the two of us—Mica and me. Cody was in the store with Mom, helping himself to postcards. Aunt Emma had told him he could have one of each kind. Out front, Mr. Frosty was packed and ready, prow pointed toward the road.

I could see Dad and Uncle Bert on the back deck of the store, elbows on the railing. They were having that last conversation adults have to have before going their separate ways. Uncle Bert laughed, then slapped Dad's back. Dad pushed the bill of his baseball cap up and looked our way.

"Better do it if we're going to," I said.

"Wait!" said Mica. I had been ignoring the small wrapped bundle in her hand, afraid it was some kind of mushy present. She grabbed my wrist and dropped it on my palm. "Give this to Anna, okay? And don't crush it."

I looked at the folded piece of paper. It was fat in the middle, but weighed hardly anything. "What is it?" I asked, closing my fingers.

"Don't squeeze!" She pinched my arm. "It's delicate. It's a letter with a janthina shell in it. A specimen. Tell Anna that the janthina is a traveler that lives on the surface of the water. Tell her that it blows across the ocean. That's why the shell is so thin and light. Tell her all that, and don't break it, understand?"

"Sure. Okay." I set the little package on top of a piling. "Now, how about that swim?"

She snatched the package off the post. "Don't put it there! It'll blow down." She tucked it carefully inside one of the sneakers Mom had left on the dock for me when she closed up the last suitcase. "And don't shove your fat foot in unless you take the shell out," said Mica. "Don't forget."

"I won't." I planned to keep my shoes off as long as possible. But colder weather a little way up the state would force me back into them. I wouldn't have time to forget.

Slip landed on the dock in front of the store. Dad stretched. Any second now he would call, "Ben? Time to go, bud."

"Come on, Mica, let's hit it." I took a couple of running steps across the dock.

Mica grabbed my arm before I could jump. "It's the last, last swim, Ben. You can't just jump."

"No? And how am I supposed to get in?" But I already knew.

Halfway up I closed my eyes. The mast swayed and I held onto the ropes. It was like I was at sea again where the motion went on hour after hour.

We hadn't motored into Bert's Marina until two A.M. The search had taken that long because Dad and Dr. Delano combed the creek and some of the bayside in the *Lazy Afternoon*. I wondered if they had done the whole thing without talking after the blowup over the AA brochures. When they came back empty, Uncle Bert had shouted to a guardsman across the canal. By the time he and Mom left the dock in a Coast Guard patrol boat, our two fathers had been sweeping the oceanside for half an hour.

Aunt Emma, Communication Central, manned the phone and the radio, mobilizing the members of their boating club. All together there were fourteen boats looking for us. It would have been cool to be picked up by the Coast Guard, but I was glad it was our fathers who had found us.

When we got back to the houseboat Aunt Emma wrapped us in blankets. Mom gave us mugs of hot soup, crying the whole time. I said how sorry I was and told her she might want to keep her eyes open for a better big brother for Cody. She just hugged the air out of me.

"Hey! You up there. Quit stalling," Mica called from the deck of the sailboat. "Get on the spreader and jump."

I shinnied up the last few feet and stood on the bar that kept the ropes apart. I held the mast tight and felt my heart pound. I hate heights. But when would I have a view like this again? Seeing the tar roof of the store for the first time, I thought how small it looked. It was littered with fish bones dropped by feeding ospreys.

Dad, in his Key Weird T-shirt, shaded his eyes and looked up at me. He waved. I waved back. Slip spread his wings and flew.

I turned toward the ocean. From my perch I could look over the road and the bridge and see the Atlantic, sparkling like chrome. I counted four sails and three powerboats. The speeding powerboats left streaks of white foam like jet contrails in the water. I breathed deep and smelled salt and the low-tide stink of seaweed drying on the flats. Across the canal the Coast Guard flag snapped in the wind.

"Coming up," Mica warned, grabbing a rope. "If you don't jump soon, I'm going to charge rent."

"In a second. I'm looking around." On the deck below I saw the shadow line at the edge of the hatch that covered the rope locker where the tarp and wood had been stowed the first day we were here. The scooter leaned against a piling. Aunt Emma was peeling the shiny paper off the door of the houseboat, taking down Christmas. Mica tapped my foot. She was just below me on the mast. "Any advice?" My throat was getting tight. The water was a long way down.

Holding a rope, she leaned out. "You see that dark spot? The water's really deep there. Aim for that and be sure you jump clear so you don't hit the bow rail or anything. And whatever you do, don't belly flop."

"Good tip." I could feel my heartbeat in my left eyelid, ticking away. Sure, I was scared, but after all we'd been through, what was the worst that could happen? Mica'd have to rescue me. And was I going to let that happen?

Fat chance.

I pushed away from the mast and jumped. As the air whistled by my ears I let out a yell. I wanted to tell Cass, people *can* fly.

The water hit the soles of my feet a hard slap, like something solid, and then I was plunging through crackling water going down, down, swallowed by darkness. I forced my eyes open. Way above my head was the mirror surface of the water. I kicked hard and broke through the mirror into the air. I let out another whoop, then shook my head to get the water out of my eyes and looked up.

Mica stood on the spreader. She looked small, like a bird silhouetted against the rising sun. She raised her scrawny arms over her head slowly—and flew. This time I clapped when she surfaced. "Great dive," I said.

"Easy cheesy. You could do it too if you lived aboard and spent all your time sailing around." Then she did a double back roll, the print on her suit flashing.

"Ben," Dad shouted. "Time to head-em-up and move-em-out, buddy."

Mica latched onto my arm so I had to drag her back to the dock. "Don't go, Ben. Don't go."

"You know I have to."

She was still attached to my arm when I hosed off. I held the hose over both of us. Water dripped off her eyelashes, but she never closed her eyes. "You gotta let go, Mica. I mean it. I have to go home."

Her fingers slid off my arm. On a dry patch of dock she drew a line with her wet big toe. I noticed that the chip of polish was gone.

"Are you going to be okay?" I hesitated. "With your dad, I mean."

She put her hands on her skinny hips. "And why wouldn't I be?"

"I don't know." I wanted to say because of his drinking, but I didn't. The whole thing was none of my business, but like Dad, I couldn't leave it alone. I was worried about her. "I just hope your dad spends a little more time with you."

"You think I can't take care of myself?" But she knew what I meant. She pushed her wet bangs back with her wrist, then looked away. "We talked about it a long time last night. He says he'll stick closer to home. We have a 1000-piece puzzle and we're going to do it together—a picture of the Alps."

"The Alps. Sounds great! Now, would you quit looking so pathetic?" I said.

"Who are you calling pathetic?"

She tried to grab the elastic on my trunks, but I gave her the slip. I dodged into the houseboat to put on the change of clothes I'd left out. When I went into the kitchenette for a plastic bag to put the suit in, I could see Mica out the window. She stood with her arms wrapped around herself, staring at my shoes. Her bare foot tapped the one with the shell in it, then she turned and walked quickly down the dock.

chapter twenty-eight

CASS

I should've seen it coming. We were having the big good-bye scene. Mica kissed Mom and Dad like they were a favorite aunt and uncle. She kissed the top of Cody's head—even though he told her he didn't want any girl cooties. Then she lunged at me. Luckily, she was too short to nail me on the lips. Instead she got the side of my chin, planted a juicy one.

"Jeez, Mica!" I twisted away. But then I gave her a quick hug. "I'm gonna miss you." I don't know what came over me—maybe it was sitting in the Zodiac with her, waiting to die—but that's what I said. And I meant it.

"Here's our address." Mom pressed a piece of paper into Mica's hand. "Any time you're up our way, come visit. We're always home."

"*Always* home," Cody repeated.

Dad and Uncle Bert bear-hugged, slapping each other's backs, then Dad held out a hand to Dr. Delano. "You take care," he said, trapping Dr. Delano's hand in both of his and staring into his eyes. Dad was lasering a message at him: quit drinking, be a good father, pull yourself together. Trust me, Dad can say plenty without opening his mouth. When he'd burned the message in good, he turned to me and Cody. "You ready, boys?"

"Wait," Mica yelled. "I need a picture for the wall." While her dad fished a camera out of one of his buttoned pockets, she hung an arm over each of our necks. She pulled Cody up and me down until our cheeks touched hers. I was yelling "Help!" when her father pressed the button. In a few days we'd be hanging goof-faced with the rest of her instant friends. Would she remember our names in six months? I mean, without reading the caption? I hoped so.

Still buzzing from all the kissing and hugging, Cody and I piled in back. "We ride!" Dad shouted. Aunt Emma and Uncle Bert waved like mad. Mica waved once, then turned and buried her face in her dad's shirt. He put his arms around her and held on. She'd scared him getting lost at sea, and he still looked scared. I just hoped he wouldn't forget and get unscared, and slide back. A person can't go around risking her life all the time just to get a little attention.

Dad let a pickup with a jet ski in back pass, then he hit the gas and turned left. The dust cloud that had followed us in trailed us out as we left Bert's Marina. So did the jingly recording of "Mary Had a Little Lamb."

We were back on US 1, a highway I knew ran all the way up the coast to Maine, a trip I'd like to make sometime. But for now, we weren't going that far. For now, we were headed home.

Cody and I slept a lot on the drive back to Tallahassee, Mom too. Dad guzzled coffee out of Styrofoam cups and sang along with the radio to keep himself awake.

Each time we stumbled out of the van at a rest stop, the air was cooler. I stuck Mica's note in the pocket of my T-shirt and put my sneakers on. With each passing mile the Keys receded, shrinking until they seemed as small and flat as one of the island stamps in my collection.

Even though I'd washed it a couple of times, I could still feel the place where Mica had kissed me. It felt all dried-spitty.

Up around Lake Okeechobee Cody said, "Scoot over. I want to look at my postcards all together." As he put them down in careful rows I remembered Cass's postcard. The one I *hadn't* sent her. This is bad, I thought.

"Say, could I have one of those cards, Cody?"

But Cody didn't want to part with even one. "I have twenty-seven, and they're all mine."

"Come on, bro, share."

"No way."

I tickled him until he couldn't get his breath. "Give it!"

"Stop, Ben!" He slapped at my arms. "I'm gonna pee my pants."

I sat back. When all else fails… "Wait, did you say you have twenty-seven cards?" He nodded. "That's too bad."

He looked suspicious, but he bit. "What's too bad about it?"

"Twenty-seven's an odd number. Everyone knows that's bad luck. I could take one off your hands and then you'd be okay."

"Why would I be okay?"

"Because then you'd have twenty-six. And twenty-six is even." I had just made that stuff up, but he believed me. There are advantages to being the big brother.

"And even is good luck," he said. "Okay, but I get to choose it out." He picked up a card, put it back down, reached for another one, and grinned. "Here."

"That one? You sure?"

"Yup, I'm sure."

It was twilight when we pulled into the neighborhood. Everything looked the same, but I felt like I'd been gone for a couple of years instead of a week and a half. We were passing the Bodine's when the Christmas lights came on. I ignored the blinking and flashing and tried to catch a glimpse of Cass through the front window. I could see their tree—they put it up early and take it down late. No Cass though. Looking for her, I noticed that my chest hurt. I wondered what a heart attack felt like, and if you could have one before your fourteenth birthday.

Next door, Jemmie's grandmother was rocking on the porch, her black sweater bundled around her, just like I'd imagined. "Nana Grace!" Cody shouted. "It's Cody. Remember me?"

"Now how could I forget you, child?" Nana Grace called back.

When we climbed out of Mr. Frosty the breeze smelled like pine straw and damp earth. It was nothing like the salt and seaweed wind of the Keys; it smelled like home.

It got dark while we unloaded. Streetlights came on. "I have to go see someone," I said.

"I hate to have to remind you, but you're grounded," Dad said.

I picked up another suitcase. "Can't the grounding start tomorrow, Dad? Please? It's important."

He stared at me for several seconds, then nodded. "Get the grunt work done first, then you can go."

Finally, when all our junk was in the house, I bent the postcard and slid it into the back pocket of my jeans and went out the door. My bike was right where I'd left it against the house. So I wouldn't wreck the card, I pedaled standing up.

The first thing I saw was Anna and Beauty in the middle of the street. "What're you doing?" I asked, dragging my foot to stop the bike.

"We're observing the full moon." The legs of the tripod scraped as she moved it a few inches. "I got this great telescope for Christmas. Want to see?"

Now that I was actually headed for Cass's house I felt nervous. So when Anna stepped back I wheeled over and put my eye to the eyepiece. "It won't be full until tomorrow night," I said, remembering what Mica had told me while we waited to be rescued or die.

"True." Anna sounded surprised that I knew.

I studied the craters for a few seconds, but I couldn't dodge it. There was something I had to do here on the home planet. "Nice scope," I said. I turned the front wheel, then remembered the note in my shirt pocket. "Hey, Anna, I have a letter for you."

"You do? Who from?"

"A girl who was staying at the marina. She lives aboard a sailboat and travels around with her dad. She goes to school by mail. Her name is Mica."

"She lives on a boat? Cool."

I put the little package in her hand. "Now don't go squeezing it," I warned. "There's a fragile shell inside. A janthina. Tell you more about it later. I gotta go." Now that I didn't have to worry about breaking the shell, I moved the postcard to my shirt pocket and put a foot on the pedal.

She had started opening Mica's letter, but stopped. "Where are you going, Ben?"

"Gotta see somebody." I stood on the pedals.

"Thanks for the letter," she called. "And the shell. Say hi to Cass."

I kept pedaling. How much does she know? I wondered.

As I passed Mr. Barnett's, his upstairs light went out. It was getting late. If I was going to see Cass I had to get to her house before her dad locked up.

Nana Grace was still rocking in the yellow glow of the porch light. "Good trip, Ben?"

"Yes, ma'am." I pedaled slow, past Cass's house then back.

"How'd Santa treat you boys?" Nana Grace asked.

"We each got a new rod and reel, and scooters."

"My, my." She shook her head, watching me circle. "You boys must'a been awful good."

I made a figure eight in front of the Bodine's, looking up at the windows. I was pedaling so slow it was hard to keep the bike from falling. "Getting kind of late to be sitting out," I called to Nana Grace. "Chilly too."

She sighed. "Just looking at old man moon. But it *is* getting kinda nippy." She stood. "Well, believe I'll go inside. Good night, Ben."

"Good night, Nana Grace. And happy New Year."

"Same to you," she said. "And Ben?" She had the door half open, but turned back. "Go ahead and knock. She'll be glad to see you."

My face felt hot. Did anyone *not* know? And if everyone knew, her father knew. And if her father knew—I was dead meat. I leaned my bike against the fence so it pointed toward the street—I could be out of there quick if I had to—and I started up the walk.

I could just see the spot where our handprints were, a dark shadow in the middle of a lighter one. You better believe I stepped on them. About to knock on that door, I needed all the luck I could get. But I never got to knock, because as I reached the stoop, the front door opened, just a little, and Cass slipped out. She put a finger to her lips, then turned the knob so it wouldn't click when she closed it. She stood on the top step. I knew I was supposed to say something, but I choked.

"Hi, Ben." My name sounded different when she said it this time. Heavier. More important.

"Hi, Cass." I tried to make her name sound heavy too. "I guess Anna called you." She nodded. I wasn't surprised. Girls are connected by telephone wires.

When I got up next to her, I smelled perfume and the smoke from her dad's cigarettes. Her hair was loose, like in the picture. I was kind of glad she was wearing a big sweater. I didn't want to stare at her boobs. In the blinking light I caught the flash of a silver chain around her neck.

"You just get back?" she asked.

"A little while ago. My parents made me help unload the van."

She sat down on the step. "I guess you *did* get here ahead of the postcard."

"Actually," I said, sliding the card out of my pocket, "we got here at the same time." I sat down and handed it to her.

She looked at the card in the flashes of red and green from the Christmas lights. "What's it of?"

"Read the caption."

"The Florida Keys at night." It took her a second to realize that she was looking at a totally black card with nothing on it but the words. "Very funny." She gave me a quick punch on the arm.

"Hey," I said, snatching her fist out of the air. We'd done this a million times before, only this time I didn't let go, and this time she didn't make me. Me holding on, her not pulling away, we both breathed hard, like we'd been running. It could've been me, but I think it was Cass who made the first move. Somehow we went from horsing around to holding hands. "How'd you do at the Jingle Bell Marathon?" I asked, like this was a normal situation, us holding hands.

"Third. I won coupons for two free pizzas at Hungry Howie's."

"Pizzas. That's good." I couldn't concentrate. Her fingers were warm and extra real.

"Jemmie and me used one coupon. Maybe we can use the other one sometime."

"In a month," I said. "Starting tomorrow, I'm grounded."

"For what?"

"For almost killing off Cody." She didn't ask how. She was there a couple of other times I'd come close. What she didn't know was that this time it was for real.

"By the way, thanks," she said, staring into the street. "For the necklace, I mean. I'm sorry, but Lou went and told everybody."

"Your dad too?"

"I guess."

"Oh." Definitely dead meat. "Thanks for the pictures. Bet your mom killed you for cutting them up."

"No." She turned and grinned. "But she will. Soon as she finds out. I hope you're worth it, Ben Floyd." She studied me like she was checking to see if being away had changed me any. "Did you have a good time down there?" she hesitated. "Any adventures?"

"It was okay. A few things happened, not much."

She touched the Band-Aid on my cheek. I didn't want to explain, so I just shrugged.

That's when I noticed that our faces were getting closer together although neither one of us seemed to be moving.

Cass's two eyes were melding into one, which is probably why people close their eyes to kiss. My heart banged against the inside of my chest. I was about to kiss a girl. On the mouth. Hoping I was on the right course, I closed my eyes.

I heard the door open. "I see the Floyds are back," Mr. Bodine rasped. While he turned to cough, we sprang apart. Cass dropped my hand.

"Yes sir, we're back." My voice cracked.

He looked from me to Cass, back and forth. "Getting pretty late for stoop-sitting, don't you think?"

I stood up fast, ready to run, then he held the door open. "Long as you're here, you may as well come in a minute and see the tree and all the other decorations. The whole shooting match comes down tomorrow. What'd your folks decorate this year?"

"Oh, the usual," I said, because I knew he got a kick out of it.

His shoulders jerked in a dry laugh, then he called, "Laura, come see what the cat drug in."

Mrs. Bodine came out of the kitchen wiping her hands on a towel. "Why, Ben, what happened to your cheek?"

"Just a dumb accident."

"Thank God it wasn't your eye," she said. She leaned down to pick up the last present under the tree. "Give this to your mom." It had to be cookies. It was cookies every year.

"Thank you, ma'am." Now that I had the cookies I knew it was time to go. "Nice tree," I said, buying a couple more seconds.

"I'll walk Ben out," Cass volunteered.

"He knows his way to the street," her father said.

So we said our Happy New Years in front of a whole audience of Bodines. "See you in school," she said, as her dad closed the door.

That was how I almost, but never quite, got to kiss Cass on the first day of the New Year. Just like I could feel the place where Mica had actually kissed me, I could feel the kiss that had almost happened, like a tingle on my mouth.

As I walked away I thought, I'm going to get that kiss. Soon.

I put my sneaker down on our lucky handprints, just to make sure.